Season Of Sin

Kylie Kent

ISBN 13: 978-1-923642-07-2 (ebook)
978-1-923642-08-9 (paperback)

Edited By
Kat Pagan

Chapter One

Hayley

I s there a worse place to be than the airport a few days before Christmas? I shuffle my way through the crowds, struggling with my over-sized suitcase and my smaller carry-on.

It'll be worth it, I tell myself when a stranger knocks right into me without even a "sorry."

Once I'm on that plane, my week of bliss can begin. I've been dreaming about this holiday all year. Literally, I booked the trip on a whim on New Year's Day. I needed to do something for me, something that I've always wanted to do. And spending a week in a tiny little European town is just what I need.

I can already picture the snow falling, walking through the Christmas markets with a hot drink. The charm, the lights, the music, the magic of the season. Sure, I'll be alone, but I'm okay with that. I don't need anyone to entertain me. I'm plenty good company.

When I get to the United Airlines check-in counter, I join the end of the mile-long line. My gaze falling on the nonexistent business class section next to me. And I can't help but wonder what it would be like to be able to afford that kind of luxury. Not having to stand around for an hour or more would be worth it.

That's not going to happen on a hairdresser's salary, though. I'm okay with economy. There was a time in my life where even the cheapest flights to Europe were a dream. I smile. I'm really doing this. Nothing is going to bring me down.

While I'm waiting in line, I go over the mental checklist I always have. I locked the house. I left enough food in the freezer and fridge for Riley. I tried to convince my baby brother to come with me, but he wasn't having it. He was adamant that eighteen was old enough to stay home alone for Christmas.

I feel bad. I'm supposed to be there for him. At the same time, it was his choice not to come. I was going to work extra shifts and scrimp on things to get him a ticket.

Ever since our parents died in a car accident a few years ago, it's just been the two of us. I never planned on becoming responsible for another whole person at the age of twenty. But Riley was only fifteen, so I *didn't* have a choice in that. It was either he moved in with me, or he ended up in a foster home.

On the day of the funeral, I promised Mom and Dad that I would always be there for Riley, that I'd look out for him. That I wouldn't let them down.

Again, guilt eats at me. I shake it away. He is going to be fine. He's not a kid anymore. Right?

Shit. I pull out my phone and call my best friend. The sister I never got but always wanted.

"Shouldn't you be catching a flight right about now?" Jade answers.

"I'm checking in. I just wanted to make sure you're going to stop by the house and look in on Riley tonight?" I ask her.

"Hayley, Riley is a big boy. He will be fine. You need to enjoy yourself, meet some sexy German hunks who will whisper dirty things to you in a language you don't understand. I mean, who cares if you don't know what they're saying? It's still hot." She sighs. "I should have come with you."

"It's not too late," I tell her, wishing there was even the slightest possibility. Jade is six months pregnant. She's not flying anywhere.

"I think it is for me." She laughs. "But I promise to look in on Riley, make sure he's not throwing ragers and all that. All *you* need to worry about is having fun. And lots of dirty sex with those hot German hunks."

I don't tell her that I don't actually find the German language sexy. If anything, it scares the crap out of me. Everything sounds so... angry.

"Okay, thank you. I love you, and kiss your belly for me. Tell my niece I love her."

"Sure, I'll do that." Jade laughs again. "Love you too, babes. Go have fun."

Pocketing my phone, I look at the line ahead of me. Only ten people to go. The closer I get to that counter, the more nervous I am. I've never been overseas. I've never been anywhere other than Miami—where I was born and raised. Why on earth did I pick some place so far?

I close my eyes and take a deep breath. *You can do this, Hayley. You've got this.* I repeat the pep talk over and over in my head.

"Next." The lady at the counter waves me forward.

"Hi, I'm going to Germany." I smile at her.

"Passport?" she asks.

"Right, sorry." I dig through my bag until I find my little blue booklet and pass it over the counter.

"What city are you flying into?"

Before I can answer the woman, my phone rings. "I'm so sorry," I tell her as I glance at the screen. I see my brother's name and silence the call. I'll call him back as soon as I'm done checking into my flight. "Ah, Munich," I reply, "I'm going to have a white Christmas."

She gives me a look that tells me she really doesn't give two shits what kind of Christmas I'm going to have. Then I'm handed a ticket and told to put my luggage on the conveyor belt. After watching my bag disappear, I head towards the departure gates. I still need to get through TSA.

Before that, I pull out my phone again and call Riley back.

"Hayley, thank god! Are you still at the airport? Did you leave yet?" he asks me, sounding panicked.

"Not yet. Why?" I tell him. "I just checked in."

"I messed up, Hay, like really bad," he says.

I groan. Of course he messed up. It's what he does best. "Riley, what did you do?"

Chapter Two

December is the busiest time of the year for me. My nightclub, Pulse, is the hottest spot on the Miami strip. Our December event space is booked out three years in advance. Not to mention all the tourists and locals wanting to get together and let loose for the holidays.

Tonight is no different. The place is fucking packed from wall to wall. I look down at the crowd from where I'm standing on the third-floor balcony.

"Good night?"

My head turns and I smile when I see Colton, my second in command, who also happens to be my best friend.

"It is." I nod. "Everything set for the meetup?"

Pulse is my baby, my legitimate baby that I use to launder the dirty money we bring in from other... less-legitimate ventures. Tonight, I'm meeting with a cartel boss to secure a coke deal that will increase our profit margins by a quarter. And when you're already working in the millions, a quarter increase is a fucking lot of money. I need this deal to go through without any hiccups.

"Everything's in place," Colton says. "You look like you need a drink *or* some pussy. You're wound far too fucking tight." He slaps a hand down on my shoulder.

Right now, I'd take either. I try to remember the last time I got laid, and when I realize I have to think about it, I know it's been way too fucking long. I don't do dry spells. I do busy spells. I've been working day and night and haven't had time to indulge.

"Let's get a drink," I tell Colton, knowing if I were to choose option number two, it'd be an all-night event. I am not some two-pump chump.

As we make our way down to the lower floor, where most of the patrons hang out, the crowds disperse, mostly because the two security guards I have walking in front of us are shoving everyone out of our way. And partly because when they do bother to look up, they see me stalking towards them.

It would be easier to have a drink in my office or on the VIP floor. I like coming down here, though. I like being seen. It deters the fuckers who are stupid enough to try to do anything in my club. It works for the most part. But every now and then, I have to make an example.

I don't let my own drugs come into this club—no fucking way will I let others bring that shit in here. Like I said, this is a legitimate business. I keep it clean. Besides the dirty money I already mentioned.

When Colton and I reach the bar, two glasses of whiskey are waiting for us and two barstools are empty. Being the owner has perks.

I sit at the end of the bar, pick up the glass, and

bring it to my lips. Colton's gaze is stuck on a leggy blonde a few spots over, and I know I've lost him.

Shaking my head, I lean in and stand. "See you in a few minutes."

"Fuck off. It'll be at least half an hour." He smirks.

"Sure it will."

I laugh before making my way through the crowd to head back up to my office. Until something catches my eye. Not something, *someone*. Some fucking kid passes a clear plastic baggy to one of my patrons.

"Grab the fucker and bring him upstairs," I tell my head of security. He's never far from my back. He nods and makes a beeline for the kid.

Looks like I've just found a way to release some of this built-up tension.

By the time I've reached my office, my rage has simmered to a nice boiling point. I sit behind my desk, draw the pistol from my top drawer, and place it right in front of me. I want this little fucker to see just how much shit he's in.

Andre comes in with a skinny-ass kid struggling in his hands. His feet dragging across the carpet. I wait for Andre to place him in the seat directly opposite mine, his hand firmly placed on the kid's shoulder.

"How old are you?" is my first question, because the boy looks fucking prepubescent to me.

"E-eighteen," the kid stutters out.

"Old enough to know better, then. What the fuck were you dealing in my club?" My next question is delivered with a harsher tone.

"I-I..." He shakes his head from side to side.

"I would advise you not to lie to me, boy. The last person to do that ended up with their tongue split in two," I tell him.

"It's nothing. Just aspirin. I swear," he says.

"Aspirin?" I cock a single eyebrow. "You expect me to believe that you're selling aspirin in my fucking club?"

"Well, they don't know it's aspirin," he tells me like I'm the fucking idiot here.

"Do you know what the penalty for dealing in my club is?" I ask. And before he can answer me, I tell him, "Ten grand or two fingers. Your choice," while knowing he doesn't have ten grand or the means to pull it together.

"I... I can get you the money. I just need to call my sister," he insists, his face a few shades paler now.

He can't be serious. He's going to call his sister?

This kid is either stupid or selfish enough to drag his sister into this mess.

Curiosity more than anything else has me nodding. "By all means, go ahead. Call your sister." I gesture a hand in front of me.

When he grabs his phone and starts dialing her number, I tell him to put it on speaker. The phone rings out, and he looks at me with wide eyes.

"She will call back. She always does," he says. And he's right. A couple of minutes later, his phone rings.

"Speaker," I grunt as he goes to answer it.

"Hayley, thank god! Are you still at the airport? Did you leave yet?" he says in one long breath.

"Not yet. Why? I just checked in," a soft, sweet voice replies. She was at the airport, and he called her? *Fucking idiot.*

"I messed up, Hay, like really bad," he says.

When his sister groans through the phone, I feel it in my dick. "Riley, what did you do?" she asks him.

Chapter Three

Hayley

This cannot be happening. My heart, along with my dream of a European Christmas, turns to dust at my brother's words.

How? I've been gone for barely two hours and he's already in trouble.

"Riley, I swear to God, you better answer me right now or I will kill you myself. What. Did. You. Do?"

"Hayley, nice to meet you." A deep, throaty voice replaces my brother's. "Hayley, are you still there?" The voice repeats before I realize I'm in a daze.

"Uh, I'm here. Who is this?" I try to regain at least a pinch of my composure.

"August. I found your brother selling something he shouldn't have been selling in my club. He seems to think you're the answer to getting him out of the shit he's currently in." He sounds amused. Is this man... making fun of me?

"Where is he?" I hiss into the phone.

"Pulse—you know it?" August asks, that humor replaced by cockiness now.

Do I know it? Everyone in Miami knows Pulse. They also know who owns it. August Wade.

"No, never heard of it. Where's it located?" I deadpan, because fuck him and his arrogance.

A deep chuckle vibrates down the line. "I'll send you the address. I'm going to assume you're coming to collect your brother?"

I sigh. "Yeah, I'll be there."

Damn it! I knew this trip was too good to be true.

"Any idea how I'd go about getting my suitcase

back from the airline before they send it to Europe?" I grumble into the phone, but really I'm asking myself. I don't expect an answer until it comes.

"Leave it. They'll return it to you," August says.

Leave it. Just leave my suitcase, full of all the new winter outfits I bought specifically for this trip. Sure, because I love throwing money away.

"Hayley?"

"Yeah?"

"You've got thirty minutes," he grunts, and then the line goes dead.

Thirty minutes? I'm at the freaking airport. How the hell am I going to get all the way to the strip in thirty minutes?

The guy is insane. And he has my brother. A maniac has my little brother. Shit!

I run for the exit and hail a cab. Jumping into the back seat while struggling with my small carry-on roller bag.

"Pulse... If you can get me there in twenty, I'll flash you my boobs," I tell the driver. I don't have spare cash to use as a bribe—and honestly seeing my boobs is way more worth it.

To my surprise, the cab pulls up at the front of Pulse exactly nineteen minutes later. And I'm alive, which is probably even more surprising, considering the way this dude drove like a damn madman.

Because I believe in following through on my word, I lift my top and flash the driver my boobs for five seconds. Then I throw him a twenty and jump out, dragging my bag behind me.

"Thanks!"

When I look up at the door, I see the line that wraps around the corner of the building. Yep, that is not going to work. So I walk past the crowds of people who are dressed up to the max, while I'm wearing sweatpants, a loose band tee, and a pair of Chucks. In my defense, I thought I was going on a plane.

Feeling a little self-conscious, I reach up and tug my hair out of the knot I piled up on top of my head. The long, brown, loose waves fall around my shoulders. I might look like a homeless person, but at least I look like a homeless person with nice hair.

"I need to get in there," I tell the bouncer.

"Not like that, you're not." He laughs in my face.

"August is expecting me," I say, hoping that will give him a little incentive.

"Name?" the guy asks.

"Hayley," I reply and watch as he turns his back on me and speaks into something on his wrist. When he faces me again, he opens the red rope. "Wait here a moment." He points to a spot just inside the door.

Flashing lights, loud music, and the stench of sweat assault me as soon as I step through. It's not that I don't like clubs. I just haven't really spent too much time in them. I was already responsible for Riley when I turned twenty-one, so I didn't get to experience all the partying that my friends were doing. Not that I minded. I was more focused on working and caring for my kid brother.

It isn't long after that, that a guy in a very well-fitted suit approaches me. "Hayley?" he asks with a smile that would either melt your panties or burn your ovaries.

"Yeah," I tell him. "Where is my brother?"

"Colton." He holds out a hand to me. I look at it but don't return the gesture. I'm not here to make friends.

"Where is my brother, *Colton?*" I repeat.

"Boss's office," he says. "You know, after this is over, you and I could get a drink. You look like you could use one." He reaches for my carry-on bag.

I slap his hand away. "I've got it, and I'm good. I don't drink with douchebags." I smile.

"You also look like you could use a really good fuck. I'm up for that too, you know, if you change your mind. Follow me." He shrugs and turns towards the hordes of clubgoers. And magically, just like Moses parted the Red Sea, the crowd splits off. Which makes it a hell of a lot easier to navigate my way through with this damn bag in tow.

The three flights of stairs he heads up next, not so much. But I do it, because I refuse to ask this jerk for help or owe him any favors.

Chapter Four

That same curiosity that had me going along with this little dog-and-pony show in the first place led me to then watch the cameras as Hayley followed Colton through the club. Why the fuck he made her walk up the stairs with that bag, I have no idea. Why didn't he take it from her?

I stand from my desk, step towards the door, and open it before they reach it. When my best friend goes to walk past me, I slap him upside the head.

"Ow, what the fuck was that for?" he asks me.

"Didn't your mother teach you any manners? You made her carry that thing up three flights of stairs?" I point to Hayley and the bag in her hand.

"I offered to take it. She didn't want me to." He shrugs.

"You could have used the elevator," I remind him.

"Yeah, but that would have been too easy for her." He smirks and makes himself comfortable on the sofa.

Turning my attention to Hayley now, I'm momentarily blown away. I was not expecting someone so... fucking gorgeous. Long brown hair and green eyes with a speckle of gold in them. Pouty lips, so fucking pouty I can almost imagine what they'd feel like wrapped around my cock.

Fuck.

"You made it here quicker than I thought," I say, closing the door behind her.

"I told the cab driver I'd flash him my boobs if he

got me here in twenty," she replies while her eyes are fixed on her brother, who looks like he's shitting himself. *As he fucking should be.*

"Did you?" I ask her.

"Did I what?" She turns back to me.

"Flash the cab driver your tits?" I walk over to my desk and reclaim my seat. I can't stand next to her and risk her noticing the growing bulge in my pants.

"Of course. He got me here in nineteen. So..." She lifts a shoulder.

"Colton," I grunt, and my friend looks over at me. Instead of telling him what I want him to do, I pick up my phone and send him a message.

ME:

Find that cab driver and burn his fucking eyes.

COLTON:

Why would I do that?

"Because I fucking asked you to." I glare at him before returning my attention to the woman in front of me. "Hayley, have a seat."

When Colton stands to leave, I stop him. "Actually, that can wait. Take Riley to your office."

"What? Why?" Hayley looks at her brother, the panic evident on her face.

"Because I want to talk to you, alone," I tell her simply.

Hayley ignores me. "Riley, what the hell were you thinking?"

"I just thought I could make some money, help you out a bit," the kid says.

"If I needed your help, I would tell you," Hayley huffs. She then looks to Colton. "Do not lay a single finger on my brother."

"Or what?" He laughs.

"Colton," I growl. "Now." I don't appreciate the way he's staring at her like she's his next meal. Especially when I plan to make her *my* next meal.

Once they're both out of earshot, she turns her now-icy glare on me. "What exactly do you want? Are you going to call the cops?" she asks. "He made a mistake. It won't happen again."

"No," I tell her.

"*No* what?"

"No, I'm not calling the cops," I clarify. "I prefer to deal with these kinds of matters myself."

"Okay, so what do you want then?"

"You," I say. Simple and to the point. This is not what I had in mind when I agreed to let the kid call his sister. I thought I'd get the money I asked for and he'd get to keep his fingers. But now that I've seen her, I don't want her money. I want her.

Hayley blinks at me, and then she stands, her palms landing flat on my desk. "I. am. Not. A. Whore," she seethes.

"Good to know." I smile.

"Glad we got that sorted. Now, what do you actually want?" she asks.

"You," I repeat.

"Did you not just hear me? I'm not a whore. I don't care how sexy your voice is or how pretty your face is. I don't care if your hands are big. I am not fucking you."

I have to hide my smile. Because, fuck me, is this woman cute when she's riled up. It's been a really long time since someone has held my interest for this long.

"I never said anything about fucking. *Although*, I'm not disappointed that *you* are thinking about fucking me, Hayley. I want you, for two weeks," I explain.

"You want me? For two weeks? To do what, exactly?" She quirks a brow at me.

"To be my girlfriend. In public anyway."

"Why? You can't tell me you're hard up for dates, August." She laughs.

Hearing my name slip out of her mouth makes my cock twitch. No one calls me August, no one but Colton. And yet, I liked when she said it. I wonder what she'd sound like screaming it?

"I can get dates. I don't want dates. I want a girlfriend to ward off all the... unwanted attention I get at events. It's the busiest time of the year for me, and I have a lot of engagements to attend."

"You just want me to attend *events* with you?" she asks cautiously.

"No, I want you to move in with me for two weeks *and* attend events with me," I correct her.

"Move in with you? I can't. In case you missed it, I have a little brother I'm responsible for," she huffs.

"You were just about to catch a flight to Europe for a week. You already left him alone." Riley told me why she was at the airport after I cut the call. "I'll have someone watch him, make sure he doesn't get into any more trouble," I say. "So, what's it going to be, Hayley. Are you going to be my girlfriend for two weeks?" I stand, button my jacket, and walk around the desk.

"*Or?*" she presses. "What's the other option?"

"You really don't want to know."

Her eyes widen. "Fine, I'll be your fake girlfriend for two weeks." The smile on her face should scare me. She looks almost giddy. "But don't say I didn't warn you."

"Warned me about what?"

"I'm not a good girlfriend, August. There's a reason I'm single." She shrugs. "Guys can't handle me."

"I'm not like other guys." I have no doubt I can handle whatever this little woman tosses my way. "Andre," I call out, knowing he is standing right outside the door.

"Boss?" he asks, popping his head into the room.

"Escort Miss Bell and her brother home. She has thirty minutes to pack her things and then escort her, alone, to my penthouse," I tell him.

"Sure thing, boss." Andre nods at Hayley. "Miss Bell."

"Wait, thirty minutes? I need more than that," she says.

"Forty," I tell her.

"An hour," she counters.

I hold her glare for a moment. Then I wave a dismissive hand. "Fine. Andre, one hour, but you're not to leave her house, and you're going inside with them."

Chapter Five

Hayley

An hour. Pack to go live with a stranger and be a fake girlfriend in an hour. I almost laugh. It's that hysterical.

"Hayley, I'm sorry." Riley is standing at my bedroom door. I haven't spoken to him since we left

Pulse. I'm devastated that he had to go and ruin my trip.

I know it's not fair. He didn't purposely ruin it for me. But he still ruined it. Which is why I haven't said a single word to him. I don't want to say something I can't take back. He is my only living family. It's just me and him. We have to stick together, no matter what.

"Hayley, just yell at me," Riley says.

"What the hell were you thinking? What am *I* thinking?" I set the lacey black bra back in my drawer and pull out some sports bras. I'm not going to try to look good for him.

"Why are you packing?" Riley asks.

"Because I have to go and live with that asshole for two weeks. I have to be his fake girlfriend to get you out of the trouble you got yourself into."

My brother's face pales. "No." He shakes his head. "You don't have to do that. I'd rather he just take two of my fingers like he said he would."

"What?" I drop everything I have in my hands onto the bed.

"He said I had to pay him ten grand or he'd remove two of my fingers," Riley clarifies.

"Yeah, well, I guess he doesn't want your fingers

or the ten grand now. He wants me." I stab at my chest.

"Hayley, stop. We can run. We can go to the cops. I'm not letting you sleep with him to get me out of trouble," Riley says.

My face scrunches up. "I am not sleeping with him. He just wants a fake girlfriend to attend some events on his arm or something."

"Oh, well, that's not that bad. Just go to some parties for two weeks." Riley nods, like it's not a big deal.

"Argh! Riley Bell, you're going to go and stay with Jade. You are going to do everything she tells you to do. And I mean *everything*. If she wants you to rub her swollen feet, you better well rub them." I point at my brother. "You got it."

"Yes." He nods again.

Once I finish packing what I think I'll need for the two weeks, I call Jade.

"Hello? You have cell service on a plane?" she asks me.

"I didn't get on the flight," I say, plopping onto my bed.

"Why?"

"Riley." I sigh. "He got caught selling aspirin at a nightclub. I had to go and bail him out."

"Selling aspirin?" She laughs.

"He was passing it off as drugs," I explain. "Have you heard of August Wade? The guy who owns Pulse?"

"You mean the guy who owns *Miami*? Who hasn't heard of him?"

"He caught Riley. He wants me to go and live with him for two weeks and pretend to be his girl-friend," I groan, and Jade gasps.

"And you agreed to that?"

"What am I supposed to do? I can't just leave my baby brother with that monster," I tell her.

"I'm going to murder the little shit," she hisses into the phone. "Hayles, you don't need to do this. We can think of another way."

"There is no other way." I sigh.

"So, you're just going to swap a season of joy for a season of sin?" she asks me.

"I'm not sinning." I lift a shoulder, even though she can't see me.

"Oh, honey, getting into bed with a man like August Wade is the most delicious sin there is," she says.

"How would you know? Have you fucked him?" I'm almost jealous at the thought. *Almost.*

"No, but I've seen pictures of him, and a man

who looks like that knows how to sin in all the right ways." She laughs.

"Okay, gross. I've told him under no circumstances am I sleeping with him. And he agreed to it," I tell her. "I need you to take Riley in for two weeks, please and thank you. I'll owe you big time and he's already agreed to rub your feet." I cut the call before she can argue with me. Not that she would. Jade is my ride or die. She will do anything for me.

When I walk out to the living room, Andre is standing stiffly by the door. "Are you ready, Miss Bell?" he asks.

"No," I say, and he gives me a sympathetic look before he schools his features.

"Want me to take that for you?" He nods towards my bag, and I hand it over to him.

"Sure, thanks. I like you more than Colton. He's an ass," I grumble as I follow Andre out. "Riley, go to Jade's!" I yell into the house before closing the door. I'll text Jade later to make sure he shows up.

Andre opens the back of the car, and I slide in. He then walks around to the driver's seat. My hands are shaky as I buckle up. I can't believe I'm really doing this. Sure, August said he doesn't want sex, but once I'm in his apartment, he could do anything to me. He's twice my size, so I would have no chance of fighting him off. And now I feel like I want to puke.

"Miss Bell?" Andre looks at me in the rearview mirror.

"Hm?"

"The boss, he's not a bad man. You will be safe with him."

I laugh. "Have you read the tabloids?"

The boss is Miami's very own bogeyman, and I'm about to move into his dungeon. Okay, he did say it was a penthouse, but that's not the point.

"You should judge someone based on your own experiences with them. Not what others want you to believe about them," Andre says.

I don't reply, because what do I say to that? He's right. I shouldn't judge the guy based on gossip.

Chapter Six

I received a message from Andre letting me know Hayley was at my penthouse. I haven't been able to stop thinking about her ever since I let her walk out of my office. I wanted to tell Andre

I'd take her myself. And I would have, if I didn't have this fucking deal to handle.

"So... what's happening with the chick?" Colton asks.

"What chick?" I know who he's talking about, but I'm not going to tell him shit.

"Hayley. I call dibs, by the way," he says, nudging my shoulder with his.

I've never wanted to slit my friend's throat more than I do right now. "Are we in middle school? You can't fucking call dibs on a woman, Colt," I tell him, quickly adding, "And you're not fucking touching her."

"Why? Because you're going to?" he presses.

"They're here." I straighten my shoulders. We need to get this done. Because I have somewhere else I'd much rather be.

When the fucker steps out of his car, followed by three of his goons, he makes it one more step towards us before gunshots rain down on the deserted area.

"What the fuck?" I duck and shove Colton behind our SUV. Retrieving the pistol from behind my back, I look up. "Motherfucker!" I yell at the asshole on the roof with a semi-automatic in his hand.

I take aim and return fire. No fucking way am I

dying here. Not tonight. I manage to hit his shoulder and look around when the shooting stops.

He's alone? What kind of idiot comes alone? The same idiot trying to take out a cartel boss, apparently.

I run towards the building. It takes five minutes to make it up the several flights of stairs, with the heavy boots of Colton and a shit-load of Mexican henchmen behind me. I kick the door open and step out onto the rooftop and then I'm shoved against the wall. Something sharp pierces my left arm.

"Fuck." I push at the asshole, and then a shot's fired and he's falling to the ground, after his fucking blood and brain matter splatter all fucking over me.

"A friend of yours?" I ask Daniel Reyes. He's my current distributor.

"Friends don't usually try to kill you," he says spitting on the body between us. "Now that that's settled, let's talk business."

"I need to triple my supply," I tell him. "We're expanding."

"You got the capital to front it?" Reyes asks.

I don't answer him. Because one, the question is a fucking insult. And two, he already knows the answer.

"Okay, how do you plan on getting that in?" He cranes his head to look at me. "I had a boat seized last month. From what I hear, they're tamping down on the ports *in your city*."

"I've eradicated the problem. The port authorities just underwent a change in management and have a new rotation of staff." I smirk. I made sure my people filled all those vacant positions.

Reyes considers the offer. It's not like he doesn't have the supply. "Okay. We'll try it out. If everything runs smoothly, we can revisit terms." He holds out a hand.

I return the gesture. "Okay. But at the three-month mark, I want five percent taken off the price," I tell him, gripping his palm a little tighter.

"Do you now?" Reyes lifts a challenging brow.

"I'm giving you three times the profits, Reyes," I remind him.

"I'll consider it." He slaps my shoulder. "Sorry about the fireworks. Occupational hazard."

"Nothing I haven't seen before."

Colton and I leave the rooftop. Neither of us utters a word until we're back in the car. I throw him the keys.

"Drive," I grunt.

"You want me to get the doc to come stitch that up?" he asks me.

"Nah, I'll do it myself." I don't want anyone else at the penthouse. I just want to see her. Hayley.

When I get home, the place is eerily quiet. Like it always is. I don't know what I was expecting. I guess just more... noise.

I find out why it's so quiet when I walk into the living room. Hayley is asleep on the sofa. I stand and watch her for a moment, taking the opportunity to really appreciate her beauty.

The girl is fucking stunning.

Then I pivot and head for the bathroom. Specifically, the shower. I need to get this fucking mess off me. When I glance in the mirror, I'm glad she's asleep. I look like I just slaughtered someone. The moment I step under the water, it turns red and swirls around my feet.

I scrub myself twice. Once to get the blood off and again for good measure. The slice on my arm stings like a fucking bitch. I inspect the wound. Luckily, it's not as bad as I thought.

I get out of the shower, dry off, and then grab the

first aid kit. Settling for some butterfly stitches and a gauze pad. Once I've patched myself up, I slide on a pair of sweats and walk back into the living room. Hayley is still fast asleep.

Bending at the waist, I pick her up as gently as I can, because I really don't want to have a fight with her right now about where she is sleeping. I'll save that entertainment for the morning.

I tuck her into my bed before covering her with the blanket. She stirs a little but doesn't wake up. I switch off the light and climb in next to her. I'm fucking drained. A few minutes later, we're both fast asleep.

Chapter Seven

Hayley

There's that sweet spot between being asleep and being conscious. Everything feels so warm and cozy. I'm aware of the world around me but I'm not a hundred percent awake. That's where I am now as I snuggle deeper under the covers. I can probably get back to sleep.

That thought evaporates the moment I feel a weight on top of me. When I look down, I see one big, tattooed arm draped over my waist and my heart rate picks up.

What the hell did I do last night? Oh, right. I agreed to be the Miami monster's girlfriend.

I quickly glance under the covers and see that I'm fully clothed. Still, I let out a scream. I don't know why I do it. But instinct, fear, *something* tells me to scream. Seconds later, that tattooed arm swings off me and drops back down to the side of the monster. He's now standing at the edge of the bed with a gun in his hand.

He looks around the room, probably searching for whatever made me scream. He fails to check the mirror, though.

"What the fuck? Hayley, what's wrong?" He walks over to me, as I continue to clutch the blankets to my chest.

What's wrong? Is he serious?

"I... What am I doing here?" I did not put myself in this room. In this bed. In what I'm now realizing is *his* bed.

August's bed. AKA the monster. AKA the beautifully-sculpted monster. Nope, I am not checking out his naked torso. I don't care if he has...

Wait, is that eight? Holy shit, the guy has an eight pack. Who is he? Oh, and that delicious-looking V that disappears under the band of his sweatpants. But, again, I'm not looking.

He cups my chin, lifting my gaze to meet his. "You do remember coming here yesterday, don't you?"

There is what seems to be a genuine concern in his voice. His touch scorches my skin, reminding me that this man comes with a ticket straight to hell. That's a train I don't want to jump on, no matter how good he'd make the ride.

Damn it, Jade. This is her fault for putting those thoughts in my head. I'm not some hussy, so it's been... a really long time since I enjoyed *any rides*. I don't need them.

"I remember coming to your apartment, but how did I get here. In this bed? With you?" I ask him.

"You were asleep on the sofa," he says, as if that answers my question.

"This isn't the sofa. It's a bed."

"I know." August pulls back, seemingly happy

enough that I'm fine and there are no monsters under the bed. Just standing next to it. Then he places the gun on the dresser.

How did I forget he had *that* in his hand?

"August, did you bring me to bed?" I'm more direct this time, because something tells me this man has a way of evading questions.

"Yes," he says.

"Why?"

"Because you were asleep, and I didn't want to wake you. Would you rather I left you on the sofa?" he counters.

Leave me on the sofa, alone, instead of sleeping next to the six-two (maybe six-three) human devil god currently standing here in all his bare-chested glory. His dark hair is falling over his forehead while his brown eyes stare right into mine as if they can see into my soul, see every thought I'm having. Thank goodness he can't. This man does not need his ego stroked.

"Yes," I tell him. "I would much rather sleep on the sofa than in bed with you."

August blinks at me, clearly in disbelief. "That's the first time I've ever heard a woman say that," he mumbles. "Lucky for you, I'd never allow my girlfriend to sleep on a fucking sofa when we have a perfectly good bed right here."

"August, we agreed I didn't have to sleep with you," I remind him.

"I thought you were referring to sex, babe, not *actual* sleep." He delivers me a panty-melting smirk, complete with a little dimple in his cheek.

"I was," I admit. "But... you have a guestroom. Surely, this place has a guestroom. I'll sleep in there." I jump off the bed.

"There're no guestrooms here for you," August says.

"Fine, I'll sleep on the sofa."

August shakes his head with a chuckle. "You're not sleeping on the sofa, babe." He walks into the bathroom.

Standing up without thought, I follow him and then stop. Waiting for the sound of the toilet to flush. I walk into the bathroom as he's washing his hands.

"What do you mean I'm not sleeping on the sofa? I'm not sleeping with you," I repeat.

"We can sort this out later," he says. "You hungry?"

I'm staring at his back. Damn it. He has those two little indents right above his ass. My eyes dart upwards. He totally caught me checking him out.

"Hungry?" His voice dips when he asks it the second time.

"No." I'm actually starving. I skipped dinner last night. The gurgle of my stomach gives me up, though. When August lifts a brow at me through the mirror, I groan. "Fine, I'm hungry," I admit.

My gaze falls to his arm, to the stream of blood slowly dripping down.

"You're bleeding. What happened?" I close the distance, reach out, and take hold of his arm, turning it so I can inspect it better. There's a piece of gauze covering a wound that has clearly been ripped open. Removing the tape, I see a small slash that he's attempted to seal himself. "You need stitches."

"It seems that way," he says, looking down at me. He then opens the cabinet next to him and pulls out a first aid kit.

"What are you doing?" I ask when he removes a sterile packet with a needle inside it. He grabs for some thread next.

"You just said I needed stitches."

"Yeah, but you're not doing it yourself," I tell him.

"Are you going to do it for me, then?" August holds out the needle towards me.

I shake my head. "I can't stitch you up. I'm a hairdresser, not a doctor." This guy is out of his damn mind. "Also, you need to clean that first."

I shove him aside and fish around in the kit until I find the antiseptic and some cotton swabs.

Chapter Eight

I don't move, because I'm afraid if I do, she'll stop touching me. And that's the last thing I want. One hand holds my arm still as she wipes the orange shit all over my open wound. Stings like a fucking bitch. I keep it in, though. No way am I letting her know that she's hurting me.

"Okay, that's a bit better, I guess," she says, discarding the last ball of cotton into the trash bin next to the sink.

"Thanks," I grunt, clearing my throat. I pick up the needle that I already threaded. This isn't the first time I've stitched myself up. Won't be the last either.

"What happened?" Hayley asks, watching as I push the needle through my skin.

"I got stabbed," I tell her.

"With a knife?" Her eyes widen.

"Yes." I grit my teeth as I continue tugging the wound closed.

"Who would be stupid enough to try to stab you?"

I smirk. "I have no idea. He was there to kill someone else."

"Stop. You can't tell me these things, August." Hayley holds up a hand, and I shrug.

"You asked."

"Yeah, but you don't need to tell me." She looks at me as if I've grown two heads.

"I don't lie, Hayley. If you ask a question, make sure you really want to know the answer, because I will tell you." I have no reason to lie, and honestly, I consider it a sign of weakness.

"You're making a mess of that. Give it to me."

She snatches the needle and thread from my hand, and I watch her face as she concentrates on my wound. The needle goes through and then through again. She does some weird things with the stitch that closes the wound tighter than I could do myself.

"I thought you said you didn't know how to stitch."

"I don't, but I do sew-in weaves. Figured it can't be too different. Also, the thought of causing you pain isn't unappealing." She smiles up at me as she pushes the needle through my skin again.

I maintain my composure, even though it still hurts. "I'm not really into that kind of kink, but for you, I'd give it a go." I wink and watch her cheeks turn a nice shade of red.

It's good to know she's not completely unaffected by me. Because standing this close to her, having her hands touch me, has my cock fucking hard. I'm glad she's focused on my arm and not somewhere south, because there is no hiding the way my sweats are tented.

"Ew." Hayley scrunches up her face. "Never going to happen."

"Never say never, Hayley," I tell her. Because by the end of these two weeks, I will have her in my bed. Squirming beneath me and begging me to fill her cunt.

The needle pushes in deeper, and I flinch. *That fucking hurt.* When she smiles up at me again, I know she did that on purpose.

"There. All done," she says with a sweet voice that goes straight to my dick. She washes her hands and then walks out of the bathroom.

After cleaning up and covering the wound with another piece of gauze, I find Hayley in the living room digging through her bag.

"Looking for something?" I ask her.

"My sanity, because surely I've lost it," she replies, and I laugh.

"Pretty sure you've still got plenty of that, babe." I turn and head into the kitchen.

"It's Hayley, not *babe*. I am not your babe!" she yells at me.

"For the next two weeks, you are," I yell back. I don't get it. Any other woman would be jumping at the chance to play my fake anything. Not her, though.

I take out ingredients and start chopping a variety of vegetables to make omelets for us.

When Hayley walks into the kitchen, she looks from the counter up to my face. "Do you not own shirts?"

"Why? Is my nakedness distracting you?" My lips tilt up. Knowing how much she likes my body, I decided not to put a shirt on. I caught her looking. I want her to keep looking.

"More like it makes me queasy. What are you doing?" She gestures to the counter.

"Making breakfast."

"Vegetables are not breakfast," she tells me.

"They are when they're in an omelet," I tell *her*.

"Do you have any cereal? Lucky Charms? Froot Loops? Reese's Puffs?"

I shake my head and laugh. "Those are not cereal, Hayley. They're just sugar."

"The boxes say they're cereal, so... I'm taking that as a: *no, you don't have actual breakfast food?*" She sits on the stool opposite me. "Do you have coffee?"

"I have coffee." I move to the other side of the kitchen and turn on the machine. I'm not much of a coffee drinker, but I keep it on the rare occasion I do indulge.

I also make a mental note to stock the pantry with that sugary shit she calls *cereal*. I won't touch it, but if that's what she wants to eat, I'm going to make sure she has it available.

"You'll like this," I tell her. "Trust me. It's good for you."

"You know what else is good for me?" Hayley says.

I stop what I'm doing and look over at her.

"Not being held captive by a devil god."

"One, you're not being held captive. The door is right there. You are here of your own free will. I'm not the kind of guy who forces women to do anything. Second, *devil god?*" I smirk.

I knew she liked me. Or at the very least, she likes my body and that's all I need.

"If I leave, what happens to Riley? He said you were going to cut his fingers off." Hayley scowls at me.

"He was selling shit in my club, Hayley. Trust me, he's getting off lightly with just the fingers."

"I'm not letting you cut off my little brother's fingers," she says.

"Still a choice." I lift a shoulder. "Still not forcing you."

"Is it, though? He's my responsibility. I have to look out for him," she says.

"Where are your parents?" The kid is barely eighteen. He should be living at home with his parents. But the moment I ask the question, I regret it. Hayley's eyes water up and her face drops.

Chapter Nine

Hayley

It's a simple question. *Where are your parents?* It's a common thing to ask someone. But every time I hear it, I freeze. Because I know what's coming next. The pity, the awkward silences. I don't want this man's pity. I don't want anything from him.

"Dead," I say and then I hold my breath.

"How'd they die?"

When I look up, I find August waiting for the answer, but I don't see any pity. I don't see everything I'm used to seeing, and I'm struck by a wave of relief. "They were in a car accident. Someone hit them. They both died instantly."

"What happened to the other driver?"

"The guy ran and was never heard from again." I shrug like it's not a big deal. The truth is that I'm constantly studying every stranger I encounter. My first thought... *was it you?* "Where are your parents?"

"Dead," August replies, his voice emotionless.

"How'd they die?" I ask. Because, well, he asked me.

"My father killed my mother. I killed my father."

My eyes widen and I gasp. "August!" I shriek. "I already told you, you cannot tell me those things."

"Why?" His head tilts to the side. "You gonna go rat me out to the cops?"

"No," I blurt. "But you don't know me. You shouldn't trust me with stuff like that."

Is this man serious? Does he just spill everything to anyone? If that's the case, how has he gotten as far as he has in life? Especially in *his* kind of life.

"I know you enough. And again, you asked. I'm not going to lie to you, Hayley," he repeats.

"That would be a first," I huff. All I've ever had were boyfriends who lied and cheated. I gave up trying to find anyone decent. Not that August is decent. Far from it. Jade was right. This man is nothing but sin waiting to happen.

"You had guys lie to you? About what?"

"You know, the usual things. *You're the only one... Hayley, no, I'm not seeing her anymore... I spent the weekend at my mama's house...*" I laugh, because I fell for each and every one of these lines.

August's brows draw down. "Why the fuck would anyone cheat on you? I mean, look at you. You're a fucking knockout."

My cheeks heat up at the compliment. "Thanks, but I told you I'm not a good girlfriend."

"We'll see." August stands. "I have to get ready for work. We have dinner tonight," he says. "Andre will be downstairs to take you anywhere you want to go today."

"I don't need a babysitter."

"Actually, you do. You're the girlfriend of August Wade, babe. That comes with perks *and risks*. Risks that I'm not going to take, which means... Andre will be downstairs to take you anywhere you want to go today."

Ignoring the whole "girlfriend" thing, because I do not want to unpack why that made me feel good, I look around the open living room. "Why haven't you decorated for Christmas?"

There isn't a single thing in this apartment that would indicate the holiday is fast-approaching.

"I don't do Christmas," August tells me.

"For religious reasons? Or are you just a grinch?" I lift a brow at him.

"Neither. I don't see the point. What am I going to do? Wrap gifts for myself and put them under a tree?" He looks at me like that would be the stupidest thing to do. Except it's not. I've done it. It still feels good opening things on Christmas morning.

"Okay," I say, resigned to the fact that *my Christmas* is well and truly ruined.

August walks out, and I pick up both of our plates. I don't know what else to do so I clean the mess he left behind in the kitchen. Just as I finish putting the last dish away, he appears again. This time, he's dressed in a three-piece suit. And I realize it doesn't matter if this man is clothed or not. He looks good no matter what.

"I'll be back to pick you up at seven. Be ready," he says.

"Where are we going?"

"Obsidian. It's one of my restaurants. The mayor is hosting a Christmas party. We're invited," he explains.

"*You're* invited." I laugh. Never in my life would I be invited to the mayor's anything. Unless it was to do one of the guests' hair.

August pulls a black card from his pocket. "Take this. Go shopping. Buy whatever it is you need."

I look at the card like it's going to burn me if I touch it.

"Hayley?" August's voice has my gaze drawing up.

"Again, not a whore. I don't need your money," I tell him.

A small smile forms on his lips. I can tell he's fighting it. "*Again*, good to know. But if you're going to decorate this place for Christmas, then you're going to use my money to do it."

"You want me to decorate for Christmas? But you just said..."

"I know what I said. I'm not alone this Christmas. You'll be here, so at the very least, we should have a tree. Don't you think?"

He says "we" like *we* are an actual *we*. Not something I'm going to focus on, because he just gave me free rein to decorate his apartment. There is nothing I love more than Christmas.

"Okay. Is there a limit on this thing?" I swipe up the card and flip it over.

"No," August says, sounding like I offended him.

"Okay, well, do you have a budget? For decorations?"

"Hayley."

"Yeah?"

"We don't work with budgets. Buy whatever you think the place needs." With that, he leans in, kisses my cheek, and turns away. I'm left staring at his retreating back.

What's with the *we* thing? Either this man is completely insane or... Nope, there really is no other option. I've shacked up with a madman. Well, not exactly shacked up. I'm not sleeping with him.

I head into the living room and find my phone. It's sitting on the coffee table, plugged into a charger. Did August do that? I pick it up and see a message from Jade.

JADE:

You still alive? Was he as good as
I'm imagining he is?

ME:

Still alive, and you'll have to settle
for your imagination. I'm not
fucking the guy.

JADE:

Yet.

ME:

Ever.

Chapter Ten

Walking through Pulse during the day always has a different vibe to it. People are milling about. Refilling the bars, cleaning, and everything else that has to be done to be ready for when the doors open in a few hours.

I find Colton in his office. It's right next to mine. "I have to go over to Obsidian tonight," I tell him.

"You want me to come with?" he asks. We usually attend these events together.

"Nah, I'm taking Hayley."

Colton blinks at me. "Hayley, right... How'd that go?"

"I'm still alive." I laugh. "Hear anything more about the shooter?"

"Nope. Whoever was after Reyes, they're keeping a tight lid on it," Colton says. "You're really going along with this fake girlfriend thing? Why?"

"Because it saves me from spending the night avoiding the advances of every gold digger in attendance," I tell him.

It's not a lie. I also just wanted an excuse to keep Hayley. After these two weeks are up, I will either come up with another reason to need her around or make her fall in love with me so she doesn't want to leave.

The thought has me stilling. Fall in love with me? That's not right. I don't want love. Do I?

No, I just don't want to let her go. That's not love. That's... obsession, infatuation.

"Sure, that's why." Colton eyes me suspiciously. I'm not giving him anything, though. He knows what I want him to know. "You grab the drop this morning?"

"Yeah, three-fifty-six," he says, referring to the buy-in we collected from our dealers.

"Good." It's decent. "I need you to stick around here tonight. I'll be in late."

"Suits me. Did you see the new redhead we hired for the front bar?" he asks.

"Do not sample the staff," I warn him.

This guy is a PR nightmare. I swear with the number of girls who have quit because they caved to his advances, I'm surprised he hasn't been sued yet.

"Fine, I won't," he groans. "Lunch?"

"Let's go." I'm starving.

On our way out, my phone pings. I look at the screen and see Andre's number flash across the top.

"Yeah?" I answer.

"What color scheme do you want?" Hayley's voice washes over me.

"Color scheme? For what?"

"Christmas. What color decorations do you want in your apartment?" she asks.

"I really don't care. Whatever colors you want," I tell her.

"Well, I do. So, choose: pink, gold, and silver... or green, blue, and gold."

"Green, blue, and gold," I sigh.

"Okay, pink, gold, and silver it is. Good chat." The call cuts off.

"You look... strange.," Colton says, pointing to my face. "Is that a smile?"

"Fuck off." I wipe the smile from my lips.

"So, Hayley, huh? It's all just fake, right?" he asks me.

"Why?"

"No reason." He shrugs.

The moment I walk into my penthouse, I almost walk right back out. This is not *my penthouse*. It's Santa's fucking workshop.

"Babe?" I yell into the living room, knowing she hates it when I call her that.

When Hayley comes down the hall, I'm speechless. Gone is the mess that's now my home, and all I can see is her.

Fuck me. She's wearing a dark-purple knee-length dress. It's tight, as in I can see every fucking curve she has. The top comes down into a small V, showing an ample amount of cleavage, and the sleeves sit just off her shoulders. Her long locks are piled up on top of her head in some fancy-ass hairstyle, with loose curls hanging down around her face, and her lips are painted a shiny pale pink.

"I'm sorry it's a mess. I ran out of time. Because I had to get ready, but I will finish it tomorrow," she says.

I'm struck dumb. Too dumb to reply as I take in all of her.

"Don't move," I say, pulling my phone from my pocket. I hold it up and snap a photo.

"Did you just take a picture of me?"

"Yes."

"Why?"

"Because you look fucking breathtaking, Hayley," I tell her. "And art like that..." I point to her body. "...should be appreciated forever."

"Um... thank you," she says, a nice blush creeping up her neck.

"You ready to go?" I hold out a hand. It's taking everything in me not to pull her up against me and just fucking claim those lips of hers.

To my surprise, Hayley grabs my arm. Her tiny palm disappearing into the crook of my elbow.

"You really do look beautiful," I say, pressing the button on the wall to open the elevator.

"Thanks. What do I need to do?"

"What do you mean?"

"At this dinner, what do I need to do?" she clarifies.

"Just... be you." I shrug.

"Yeah, that's not a good idea." She laughs. "Seriously, I've never been to a party with the mayor, August. I'm more likely to embarrass you than to be the asset you seem to think I am."

"You could never embarrass me, babe." To be embarrassed, you have to care what other people think, and I don't.

When we step out onto the street, Andre opens the back door of the car. "Do you ever get to go home?" Hayley asks him.

"Yes, Miss Bell, I do." He nods his head at her.

"You work too much," she says, turning to me before she gets inside. "August, you make him work too much. Tired people make mistakes, you know."

My gaze falls on Andre and his eyes widen. "Sir, I don't complain," he says.

I slide in next to Hayley. "I know."

Chapter Eleven

I can't stop fidgeting. I don't know what is expected of me. August says to *just be myself.* The thing is, he doesn't know who I am. He's some all-important, scary leader of Miami. Me? I'm a hairdresser. Nothing special.

I managed to get lost in the shopping for Christmas decorations today. I did feel a little sorry for Andre, who had to follow me around the whole time. But he was a good sport about it, offered to carry bags for me constantly. He even kept opening all the doors, which is strange.

But as soon as I had to start getting ready for tonight, the nerves set in. My dress didn't come with a price tag on it. I picked it up on sale last season and haven't actually had any excuse to wear it. I had Andre take me back to my place to pick it up, along with some heels and a clutch. And some nicer underwear because, well, the dress deserved it.

I feel like a fraud, though. I should not be here with this man. I don't belong.

The car pulls up to the front of Obsidian, a restaurant I've heard clients rave about but never could actually afford to eat at. There's a red carpet and...

"Is that paparazzi?" I ask August, looking out the window.

"Yes. Stick close to me. Don't let go," he says in a voice more serious than I've heard from him.

I nod my head. This is way out of my element. I have no idea what I'm doing. August cups my face. I don't instantly pull away, even though I know I should.

"I would never let anything happen to you, Hayley," he tells me.

"What could happen to me?" I ask, my nerves going into overdrive.

"Nothing, because you're going to be right by my side, and Andre will be right by your other side," he says as the door opens.

August steps out and literally blocks the exit for what seems like five minutes before he moves aside and holds out a hand for me to take.

"I was starting to think you changed your mind and were going to let me stay in the car." I laugh.

"And miss having the most gorgeous woman in Miami on my arm? Never." He smiles at me, and some of my nerves are replaced with butterflies I have no business feeling.

I grip August tight, afraid that if I don't, I'm going to get separated from him. Which is what I'm supposed to want. *Damn it.*

The moment we step onto the red carpet, all the flashes blind me. "Holy shit," I whisper.

August drops my hand and wraps an arm around my waist. "It's okay. I've got you," he says into my ear before kissing the side of my head. "Just smile."

Smile. I can do that, without looking like someone who just escaped the psych ward. Hopefully.

August stops in the middle of the carpet. A chorus of people shouting his name and firing different questions at him. Then I hear the one I was dreading the most.

"Who is your date, August?"

I cringe.

"My girlfriend. Hayley." August smiles widely before he turns to me, cups my cheek, and stares into my eyes. "Ready?"

Ready? For what? There's more?

His lips lower onto mine. His tongue pushes into my mouth. And all the noise fades away as he kisses me. No, he's not just kissing me. He's possessing me.

When he pulls away again, his thumb wipes along my bottom lip. "Let's go in," he says, leading me into the building.

"What the hell was that?" I hiss under my breath.

"That was the first fake kiss of our fake relationship, babe."

Nothing about that kiss felt *fake.*

The moment we enter the room, August starts getting bombarded by men who all want a little bit of his time. He introduces me, always smiling down at me like I really am his girlfriend and he's so damn proud to have me on his arm.

I've never had a real boyfriend look at me the way August does. It's strange. But I don't hate it. I just have to keep reminding myself who he is and why I'm actually here. *To stop him from cutting off my little brother's fingers.*

That thought sobers me up, and my body stiffens.

August notices. He holds up a hand to stop whomever's talking to him and turns his full attention to me. Stepping in front of me, he blocks the other men from my view. "What's wrong?" he asks quietly.

"Nothing." I shake my head.

"Something happened. Just now."

"I'm fine, and you're being rude to your friends," I tell him.

"They're not friends, and I don't care." August turns back and says, "Excuse me, gentlemen. Hayley and I are going to find our seats."

The men step aside, and I feel stupid for interrupting his conversation.

"I'm sorry," I whisper as August ushers me towards the table with his name card on it.

"For what?"

"For interrupting. You should pretend I'm not here," I explain.

August laughs. "With you, in that dress, babe, it would be impossible to pretend you're not here. And you didn't interrupt. Besides, the needs of my girlfriend trump whatever bullshit those two wanted out of me."

"Fake girlfriend," I remind him.

"Tomato, *tomahto*. Same thing, babe," he says.

Just before we reach the table, a tall blonde steps in front of August. Her hand latches on to his bicep. "Wade, it's been so long," she purrs at him. I'm surprised she isn't rubbing herself all over his legs.

The sight has me seeing red. How rude? And how dare she! As if she can't see I'm right here...

"August, babe," I say, ignoring her. My hand cups his face, angling it slightly towards me. Then I push up on my tiptoes and press my lips to his. The kiss is quick, but I think it gets my point across. "I'm going to find our table. You can catch up with your... friend?"

Chapter Twelve

I couldn't wipe the smile from my face if I wanted to. Hayley just staked her claim. Like a lioness, she saw a threat and went right for the kill. And I, for one, couldn't be prouder.

"Hayley, this is Paige. Paige... Hayley, my girlfriend." I introduce the two while shifting a step closer to Hayley, forcing Paige to drop her hand from my arm.

"Your girlfriend but, Wade, you said…" Paige looks at me with pleading eyes.

"That I don't do girlfriends. Guess things change when you meet the one. It was nice seeing you again, Paige. Say hello to Clive for me." I brush past her, with Hayley pressed firmly to my side.

We make it to the table with my name in the center and I pull a chair out for Hayley. I wait for her to sit, and then I scan the room. Once I spot Andre standing against the wall, his eyes firmly on my girl, I relax and claim my seat.

"Why does everyone call you Wade?" Hayley asks me.

"Because I don't let people call me August," I tell her.

"But I call you August and you've never corrected me." Her brows turn down.

"You're my girlfriend, Hayley. You are not just people. You and Colton are the only ones who call me August," I explain.

"Oh joy, I get to be on the same level as *Colton*," she says, her face scrunched up in disgust.

"Not a fan?" I ask her.

"The first thing he said to me was that I either needed a stiff drink or a good fuck, and he was up to give me either."

My fist clenches at my side. I should have known he'd say something like that to her. The guy can't keep his dick in his pants to save his life. "I'm sorry. He's harmless, though, and I promise the next time you see him, he will be nothing but respectful."

Because I'm going to kick his fucking ass.

I take out my phone and send my best friend a text.

ME:

I need to hit the gym, tonight. You up for sparring?

COLTON:

She told you, didn't she?

ME:

Yep.

COLTON:

See you at the gym.

The bastard knew I'd find out that he'd offered to fuck her.

"I don't need you to stick up for me, August. I turned him down. So I doubt he'd ask me again anyway," Hayley says.

"He's not used to being turned down." I laugh. "I wish I could have been there."

"I can see why." Hayley smirks. "He's hot."

"He's about to lose some teeth. How hot will he be then?" I ask her.

"I don't know. I'll have to take a look at the results. But, I mean, he's hot in the *nice to look at but I wouldn't actually touch* kind of way," she hums to herself.

Yep, I'm going to wipe that pretty boy smile from my best friend's face.

"Like you, except you're way better looking. I can appreciate that without wanting to touch," Hayley adds.

"You can touch if you want," I tell her.

"I don't," she says, her eyes scanning the room. "Oh shit..."

"What?" My gaze follows hers.

"That's Clarissa Yields," Hayley tells me.

"I know who she is."

"Did you also know she's about to leave her husband for his brother? She's been having an affair for years and is finally going to move out."

"How do you know that?" I ask, not sure if it's news or gossip. Either way, I'm curious. I do business with Clarissa's husband, Tristan.

"I cut their maid's hair. She talks. A lot." Hayley laughs. "You'd be surprised. Once someone is in my chair, it's like their lips can't stop. The stories I've heard... well, I could write a book."

"Really?" This could actually be useful. If I go to Tristan with this news, he's going to owe me a favor. Considering I'd be saving his company. Because I have no doubt that his brother and wife are scheming to take it out from under him.

"Yep. You see that couple over there. Mr. and Mrs. Bucksey, they like threesomes, but only with other men. Mr. Bucksey likes watching his wife get fucked."

I look at Hayley. "Seriously? What man would want to watch his wife get fucked by another man?"

"Mr. Bucksey, it seems." She lifts a shoulder. "Not a voyeur I take it?"

"I don't share what's mine. Ever," I grunt.

The table starts filling up with people, all of them making small talk. Hayley is silent beside me, her hands twisting in her lap.

I reach over and take hold of her palm, to stop her fidgeting and to reassure her that she's okay. Bringing it to my mouth, I kiss it before resting our joined hands on my thigh. My thumb strokes the back of her knuckles, and I'm thankful when she doesn't pull away.

"I never thought I'd see the day... You're breaking a lot of hearts tonight, Wade, including mine," a familiar voice tells me from across the table.

"Sorry, Mrs. Hughes, what can I say? I took one look at her and knew instantly I had to make her mine," I reply, my focus turning from the seventy-year-old widow to the woman beside me.

"I can see why. She's beautiful." Simon Pali, a tech guru who's come into some new money, ogles Hayley.

"And if you don't take your eyes off her, she'll be the last thing you fucking see," I growl.

Hayley clenches my hand tight. "He's kidding," she tells a now pale-looking Simon.

"No, he's not," I correct her.

The clinking of metal against glass has everyone's chatter stopping and their attention shifting to the mayor. Great, now we all have to sit through one of his boring-ass speeches.

The entire time, I concentrate on the feel of Hayley's hand in mine. How soft her skin is under my thumb as I stroke the back of her palm. On her fruity scent and the glimpse of cleavage poking out of the top of her dress.

"I really like your dress," I lean in and whisper against her ear.

"Thanks," she says, looking down at her chest.

I'd like it a whole lot better if it were on the floor of my bedroom. I don't tell her that, though, because I need to play this smart. I'm not going to pressure her to get into bed with me.

Chapter Thirteen

He left, literally walked me up to the penthouse and then said he had to go to work. I didn't argue, because I need space. He kept touching me all night, and I kept letting him.

After having a shower and changing into a pair of green silk Christmas pajamas, I lie out on the sofa. I am not getting into his bed. I'll sleep here. I don't even know if he's coming back and, honestly, I don't care.

It doesn't take long for me to drift off to sleep—not after I take a melatonin anyway.

I know the moment I wake up that I'm in his bed. At least this time I'm alone. He was here, though. I can smell him, and I didn't put myself in this bed.

I shove the covers aside and stumble into the bathroom. After doing my business and washing my hands, I splash my face and then tie up my hair into a high ponytail.

I find August already fully dressed in the kitchen. "Morning." He smiles at me. "Come here."

He holds out a hand and I blindly accept the gesture before I can think better of it.

August pulls me into the pantry. "If there's something missing, let me know," he says, pointing to the shelf that is now full of just about every sugary cereal known to man.

"Did you buy out Walmart?" I ask him. "Why would you get all these?"

"Because you asked for them yesterday and I didn't have what you wanted," he says, like that is a perfectly logical reason to go and buy over thirty boxes of different cereals.

"You didn't have to do this," I say, already reaching for the box of Lucky Charms. "But I do appreciate it. Thank you." I smile up at him.

August's gaze flicks to my lips.

Don't do it. Don't do it. Don't do it, I chant in my head, knowing he wants to lean in and kiss me.

August clears his throat, steps back, and walks out of the pantry. "Spoons are in that one," he says, pointing to a drawer behind him.

"What are you eating?" I ask as I pour my Lucky Charms into a bowl.

"Oats," he replies.

"Why?"

"Because they're good for you," he tells me.

"You know what else is good for you?" I tilt my head to the side, repeating the little game we played last time he said that.

"What?"

"Not getting stabbed with knives in the middle of the night." I smirk.

"I'll give that a go," he deadpans before holding out his spoon to me. "*If* you give this a go?"

"Pass. You can go out and enjoy some knife fights for all I care. I'm not eating that goop." I shake my head and open the fridge. I quickly locate the milk and pour a hefty serving into my bowl.

August hands me a spoon from the drawer. "I don't know how you can keep a body like *that* when you eat like shit."

"I usually go to the gym every day." I shrug.

"I own a gym. Andre can take you there if you want to use it. Not that you need to. You look fine to me," he says.

"Thanks. I think I'm going to hang here and finish decorating." I glance around at the mess of shopping bags. "We need to pick a tree. When are you free?"

"Huh?" August looks at me, clearly dumbfounded.

"To go to the tree farm. All the good ones are probably gone but they'll have something for us." I'm not picking his damn tree for him. Or is my wanting him to come along just an excuse to spend time with him?

"When would you like to go to the tree farm?" August asks.

"This afternoon?"

"Okay. I'll come back around three. Will that work?"

"Yep. Thanks." I smile, happy that he so easily

gave in. I really thought I'd have to fight him on it. With that settled, I decide to try to push my luck. "Can I invite my friend over?"

"Jade?" he questions.

"How do you know about Jade?"

"I looked into you."

I snort, knowing how dull my life is. There is something small he could have found, but I push that aside and decide to focus on the positive. "Bet that was boring as hell," I say when he doesn't bring *that thing* up.

"Nothing about you is boring, Hayley," August says, walking around the counter. "Leave the dishes. The cleaner will do them." He presses his lips to my forehead. "See you this afternoon."

"So that's a yes to Jade?" I call after him.

"It's your home, babe. Invite whomever you want," he calls back.

My home, my ass. I bet one week in this penthouse would pay my rent for the entire freaking year.

I take out my phone and text Jade while I continue to grumble to myself.

ME:

Come to the devil god's penthouse. Help me decorate.

JADE:

Devil god? So, he was good, then?

ME:

Still not fucking him.

JADE:

So… just sucking face? I saw the pictures.

Her message is followed by five images, all of me and August from last night. I save one. We look like a real couple. You wouldn't know that the kiss was fake.

ME:

Just come over.

JADE:

Be there in an hour. What's the address?

Good question. What *is* the address? I open my maps, tag my location, and then send that to Jade.

Once I finish eating, I have a quick shower, apply some light makeup, and do my hair in two braids. I pull on a pair of denim cut-offs and a band shirt before I walk out to the living room and get started on the decorations.

Jade turns up about half an hour later. With Starbucks. "Oh my god, I love you," I say, wrapping my arms around her back. Andre steps off the elevator with her.

"Miss Bell, do you need anything?" he asks.

"Want to help decorate?" I wave a hand around the apartment.

"Ah..." He looks like he doesn't know what to say.

"Relax. I was kidding. You don't have to stick around. I'm not going anywhere," I tell him.

He nods. "I'll be downstairs, Miss Bell."

"Miss Bell?" Jade bursts into laughter as soon as the elevator doors are closed and Andre is on his way back down.

"Shut it." I throw a ball of tinsel at her.

"What the hell is all this?"

"August didn't have any decorations. Like nothing. He told me to decorate." I lift a shoulder.

"You bought all this crap?" she says.

"No, *he did*."

"You guys went shopping together?"

"No, he gave me this." I pull the little black card out of my pocket and wave it in the air before tucking it away again.

"Hayley, are you sure this whole girlfriend thing is fake? Because from where I'm standing, it's looking awfully real." Jade sits on the edge of the sofa.

"Trust me, it's fake. This is August Wade. He would not want me as his real girlfriend," I assure her.

"Pfft, he would be lucky as hell to have you as his real girlfriend." Jade stands. "Okay, let's Christmas the shit out of this place. I'm loving the color scheme."

Chapter Fourteen

Sleeping next to Hayley all night and not touching her is fucking hard. It's even harder when she rolls over and unknowingly wraps herself around me. I've never been so patient in my life. I think I deserve some kind of award for my level of restraint. I had to slide out of bed early and release myself in the fucking shower like a goddamn horny teenager.

It will be worth it. I know she'll come to me eventually. She will be mine, and it'll be on her terms. Which is exactly what she needs. I could seduce her. I could have her naked within minutes and giving in to what we both want, but then there's the risk of her hating me more than she already does.

When I get home, to Santa's fucking workshop, it all finally looks organized and... not so bad. "Babe, you here?" I call out from the foyer.

"Babe?" The question comes from a voice that doesn't belong to Hayley.

"Shut it," Hayley responds as I enter the living room.

Ignoring her friend's glare, I walk over to Hayley. My lips land on her temple. "Hi." I make a point to eye her handiwork. "It looks great in here."

"Thanks. This is Jade. Jade. August." Hayley makes the introductions.

"Wade," I correct her. I was kidding when I said no one calls me August but her and Colton. "Nice to meet you, Jade. Are you coming tree shopping with us?"

"And ruin this whole Hallmark moment?

Never." Jade shakes my hand. "I'm glad I got to meet you, *Wade*. Look after my girl," Jade says and then wraps Hayley up in her arms, which turns into an awkward hug, considering the size of the woman's stomach.

I wait for Hayley to see her friend out. When she comes back, I raise a brow at her. "What's a Hallmark moment?"

"Ignore her. Pregnancy has turned her brain to mush." Hayley laughs off my question. "Are you... wearing that?"

I look down at my custom-made three-piece suit. "Ah, yeah?"

"Okay then. You ready to go?"

I then look at what Hayley is wearing. A pair of cut-offs that show her long, tanned, toned legs. Legs I want wrapped around me. "Fuck, you look good in those," I tell her and watch that familiar blush creep up her face.

I don't think this woman knows just how fucking gorgeous she is. I'll have to make it my new full-time job to tell her every chance I get until she believes it.

A few minutes later, I'm walking Hayley down to the garage. I press the button on my Audi RS, and she stops short. "Um, August?"

"Yeah?"

"This is what you want to take?"

"You don't like my car, babe?" I ask, feeling almost offended. I fucking love this car. Did I just find her first flaw?

"It's not that. It's just... how do you plan on picking up a tree? Like, we can't tie it to the roof of... this." She waves a hand towards my car.

"We have to bring it home? Don't they have delivery?"

"Um, I guess they might." Her face drops, and I instantly know she really wants to bring a fucking tree home with us.

Fuck me, what is this woman doing to me? Because now I'm thinking I need to go and buy a fucking truck just to take her tree shopping.

I look around the garage before walking up to an Escalade. "How's this one?"

"Is it yours?" Hayley asks.

"Yes." I laugh. "I'm not a car thief, babe. Come on." I walk over to the wall, where there's a safe, and enter the code. Then I switch out the keys.

Opening the passenger door, I wait for Hayley to get in. "You don't need to open doors for me," she says.

"What kind of asshole do you think I am?" I ask

her. "Don't answer that. I will always open doors for you."

I close her inside the car, walk around to the back, and text Andre to let him know what I'm driving. He'll be following us, along with two of my other men.

I'm still on edge after being shot at and stabbed the other night. And we don't know shit about the shooter or why they were after Reyes. It's crossed my mind that they weren't. Was it a coincidence the fucker started shooting when they showed up? He didn't hit anyone. You'd think a sniper would at least get one good shot in.

"What kind of tree do you want?" Hayley asks after I jump into the driver's seat and begin navigating us out of the garage. She has the biggest smile on her face.

"A Christmas one?" *Isn't that what we're shopping for?*

"When was the last time you had a Christmas tree?"

"I've never had one," I admit, because my parents couldn't afford Christmas, and when I could, I didn't bother.

"Oh my god, I'm shacking up with a grinch," Hayley groans.

"First, we haven't done any shacking up. Second, I'm not a grinch. I've just never had a reason to have a tree before."

"Christmas is the reason, August," she deadpans.

"You are the reason," I correct her. I couldn't give a shit about Christmas.

"Well, by the end of these two weeks, you are going to fall in love with Christmas." Hayley sighs wistfully. "It's the most magical time of the year."

"Is that why you were going to Europe?"

Her smile fades. "I saved all year for that trip. I wanted to experience my first white Christmas. They have the cutest little villages in Germany. I wanted snow, hot chocolate by the fire, all of that," she says.

I don't say anything, because what can I say? I'm the asshole who ruined it for her. I'm not sorry, though, because I have her for two weeks.

When we pull up to the tree farm, it looks really bare. "Are we too late?" I ask Hayley.

"We can find something," she says with determination. "We are not having Christmas without a tree. That's like a crime or something."

I laugh. "Not the worst one I've committed."

Hayley turns to me. "I don't want to know. Don't ever give me your list of sins, August. Because what if I get picked up by the cops and they want to use me against you or something? That's what happens in the movies, right? And then I'm going to have all this knowledge about things that happened. I don't want that." She's rambling.

"Babe, stop. Breathe." I take an audible breath, in and out, and Hayley mimics me. "That's not going to happen. I would never put you in a situation like that, and I sure as shit wouldn't let anyone try to use you against me. This is real life, not the movies."

"No, if it were the movies, you'd be some handsome billionaire I met by accident before we got snowed-in together in some remote cabin. One thing would lead to another, and by the end of the movie, you'd be mine." She smirks.

"You've thought about that, huh?"

"About what?"

"Me being yours? Because I'm pretty sure I know a guy who can make that happen. If that's what you want." My lips are a breath away from hers. I just need her to say yes...

"Like you said, this isn't the movies." Hayley moves back and unbuckles her seat belt.

Chapter Fifteen

Hayley

What the hell does that even mean? *He can make it happen.* If I want him to be mine, I can have him? He has to be fucking with me, messing with a girl's head just to fuck with her more. I can see him now, laughing his ass off if I'd uttered the one word that kept flicking through my mind.

Yes. I wanted so badly to just say it, but that would be stupid. I'm not here because we met at some random party and hit it off. We're not dating. We are faking it. It's all pretend. Even this whole *I can have him if I want him* bullshit. Well, I, for one, am not going to fall for it.

I'm annoyed with myself for even thinking that I could have someone like August Wade, for even wanting someone like August Wade. The guy threatened my little brother. There is something seriously wrong with me. Is it too soon for that mental illness where the captive falls for their captor?

Whatever it's called, it most certainly is too soon, and I have not fallen.

I get out of the car, closing the door a little harder than I intended. August rounds the hood, his jaw tight. "You need to wait for me to open your door," he says.

"Why?" The moment the question leaves my mouth, August's head snaps to the side and then he's jumping on me. My back hits the ground. His hand catches my head. And...

Are those gunshots?

Oh my god, they are. My body freezes.

"That's why," August grits out between clenched teeth. "Stay down." He scans our surroundings, his free hand clutching a pistol.

Where did it even come from?

When the firing stops suddenly, I feel August release a breath. He looks over at me. "You okay?"

I nod my head. "Are you?" My hands go to his chest. I don't know why, but they start roaming all over him.

"Looking for something?" August cocks a brow at me.

"Bullet holes," I tell him. "What the hell was that?"

"I don't know." He pushes to his feet. "Don't move."

I don't know where he thinks I'm going to go. My legs are numb. I'm not even sure I could stand on them right now.

"Boss, you good?" Andre walks around the front of the car.

"Yeah, you?" August asks him.

"Yep," Andre replies.

"Anyone hit?"

"Not ours."

"Any survivors?"

"One, we got him over here." Andre nods his

head to the right. I turn to look, but I can't see anything except a car tire.

"Stay with Hayley," August grunts, and then he's moving.

He's walking away. Wait! I scramble to get up. Where is he going? He can't just leave me here!

I stumble once I'm standing, and Andre catches me. "Miss Bell, are you all right?"

"Where is he going?" I ask.

"He'll be right back. Maybe you should sit in the car," Andre suggests.

I stare at him. *Sit in the car? Sure. I'll do that. Not.*

I shake my head and turn around. When I do, I see August. He's over by another car with two other men. One more is on the ground. Then I watch as August crouches down, says something, and shoots the guy right between the eyes. A scream escapes me and I fall onto my ass.

"Miss Bell, you're going to be okay," Andre says.

Am I? I knew I was living with a monster. I've heard the rumors. Damn it, he's told me the sins he's committed himself. But hearing about them and seeing them firsthand are two different things. I close my eyes and put my hands over my ears. I can feel myself rocking back and forth.

When I feel someone reach for my arms, pulling them down, I scream again. Then that someone is picking me up.

"Shh, it's okay. I'm not going to let anything happen to you." August's voice seeps through my fear-hazed brain.

I open my eyes and stare up at his face. "You... you... why?" I ask him. "You shot that man. Why?"

He tilts his head at me. "Because he could have hurt you," he says. "I won't let anyone try to hurt you, Hayley."

I shake my head. That's not why he killed him. He wouldn't kill someone because I just happen to be here. In the wrong place, at the wrong time.

The movement of the car has me sitting up. "Where are we going?"

August doesn't let me go when I attempt to slide off his lap. "Home," he says.

Home. We're not going home. We're going to *his* home. I don't bother to argue with him. What can I say? I'm literally at the mercy of a madman right now.

Even with that knowledge, my head willingly rests on his shoulder, and I close my eyes. "Who is trying to kill you?" I whisper, but August hears it. "I've never been shot at before."

"And hopefully you never will be again," Augusts says, but something tells me the longer I'm around him, the more likely it is to happen.

"I don't know. But I will find out." He presses his lips to the top of my head. "I'm sorry."

My brain is telling me that he's the reason that I was even in that situation. Still, I'm willingly taking comfort from him and a stupid part of me feels safe in his arms.

"Why would you jump on top of me, August? Someone was shooting at you. And you jumped on me. You could have been hit."

"Hayley, there is no world that exists where I would ever save myself over saving you," he says, and for a little while, I let myself believe that this could be real.

I really could see myself falling for a monster. *Season of sin.* Jade's words ring back through my mind.

"We didn't get a tree..." I mumble.

"I will get you a tree," August says, and I close my eyes again, letting his warmth wrap around me.

Chapter Sixteen

I'm going to fucking find the motherfucker who has a bullet with my name engraved on it. I had a gut feeling about that shooter the other night but figured I'd see how it played out.

Now, I know someone is gunning for my head.

Which is fine... if it were just me. But they shot at her. Hayley. And that isn't something I'm about to let go.

No, when I find out who it is, I'm going to make them fucking pay for putting her in harm's way.

By the time we get back to the penthouse, she's asleep.

"Need anything, boss?" Andre holds the car door open for me.

"Yeah, get Colton over here now," I tell him as I carry Hayley over to the bank of elevators.

She doesn't stir, not until I go to lay her on our bed. I freeze. When the fuck did it become *our* bed? She's been here for two fucking nights. I only have twelve left with her. Fucking hell.

"Where are you going?" she asks.

"I'm not going anywhere. Go back to sleep." I cover Hayley with a blanket before lying next to her on the bed, hoping she'll drift off again before Colton gets here. "I'm sorry you had to see that." My fingers brush the hair from her face.

"I think I needed to see it," she says, her voice low.

"Why?"

"To remind myself who you are, to not let myself get too comfortable here."

"Hayley, I would never hurt you," I tell her.

"As long as I don't give you a reason to," she counters. "It's okay, August. I know what this is."

"What is this?" I ask her.

"Temporary."

Leaning forward, I press my lips to the center of her forehead. "Just so you know, there is nothing you could do that would make me want to hurt you. And this is only temporary until you want to change it to permanent."

"I don't know why you've never had girlfriends before, August. You're pretty good at the boyfriend thing. It's almost believable." She yawns around her words. She's in shock. Getting shot at will do that to you.

I don't tell her that it's not fake for me. I'm not sure it ever was. I've wanted her since she walked into my office.

No, it was before that. I wanted her when I first heard her voice on the phone.

It doesn't take long for Hayley to fall asleep again. I slide off the bed, close the bedroom door, and head to my office. Before walking over to the bar where I pour myself a drink.

"I heard you caught a downpour of metal again." Colton's voice has me spinning around.

My finger comes up to my lips. "Shh, Hayley's asleep. Keep your voice down."

He looks in the direction of my bedroom. "She okay?"

"She just got shot at for the first time. What do you think?" I grunt.

"So, no." He nods. Then he walks over and plucks the drink from my hand. "This is not going to help right now," he says before downing the contents himself. "You need a clear head."

"So do you," I mutter.

"I can handle liquor better than you can, boss. What do we know?"

"Fucking nothing. I've got the IDs of the guys who tracked us to the tree farm."

"What the fuck were you doing at a tree farm?" Colton asks.

"Picking out a Christmas tree." I shrug.

"Who are you and what have you done with my best friend?"

"Fuck off. Hayley wants a tree," I tell him.

"She moved in pretty quick. This place looks like Father Christmas had an orgy in your apartment."

"It looks good. She did great. Say anything else, I'll make sure you get a matching set." I point to his face. The shiner I gave him when we were sparring the other night makes me a little happy to see.

"You really have gone goo-goo over her." Colton tilts his head at me. "You need to be certain. Like, really fucking certain before you drag some innocent woman into our world, August."

He's right. I had no business dragging Hayley down into the depths of hell with me. Now that I have her here, though, I'm not sure I can let her go. I don't know what I'm going to do after the twelve days are up.

I pull the IDs out of my pocket and toss them towards Colton. "Find out who these assholes work for. I want names, addresses, all of it. I'm going to turn this fucking city red if I have to."

"You know, it's not the first time you've had someone try to kill you," Colton says.

"It's the first time I've had something other than my own life to lose," I correct him.

"Gee, I won't take that fucking personal." He pouts.

An ear-piercing scream has us both standing and running out of the office towards my bedroom.

Hayley is sitting up on the bed. Her eyes are open but they're vacant, and the scream she's letting out could rival a banshee.

Shoving past Colton, I sit in front of her. Picking her up and settling her on my lap. "Shh, it's okay. I've got you. I'm right here." I rub my hands along her back.

"August?" Hayley looks up at me. "You left."

"I was in the office, in the room next door," I tell her.

She shakes her head. "I woke up and you left."

"I'm sorry. I'm here. I'm not going anywhere." I pull her tight against my chest and hold her like that until I feel her body relax again.

Chapter Seventeen

Hayley

I need to get a grip on myself. When I woke up and August wasn't right next to me in the bed, I freaked out. To the point I screamed, because my first thought was someone got him. That whoever is trying to kill him actually found him.

My blood turned cold.

I'm still shivering. Even now, after being enveloped in his warmth, I'm still shivering with terror. The scary thing is, I was afraid for him, not me. I need to find a shrink. Or maybe I should call Jade...

But I can't do that. What would I say? *Oh, by the way, I was shot at today?* She'd be over here in a heartbeat, threatening August with all kinds of bodily harm.

I don't need to get her mixed up in this mess. It's my mess. Well, it's Riley's mess, which I'm forced to endure yet again. Although as August's arms tighten around me and I sink farther into him, I'm not sure *endure* is the right word. I can't say I hate being this man's fake girlfriend.

I could do without the whole shooting thing, but other than that, he really has been the perfect gentleman. He hasn't pushed for anything sexual. He hasn't been harsh or cruel to me. He's been nice, oddly nice. I don't think any of my real boyfriends were this nice.

Without thought, I lift my face, shifting upwards until my lips brush his, my tongue pushing into his mouth. Not that he puts up a fight. Then I lift onto my knees, straddle his lap, and press myself even closer against him. My kiss turns hungry. I'm like a madwoman. I'm starved. I need him. My fingers tangle through his hair. It's soft, and I make a mental note to look at what products he's using.

A knock at the door has me pulling back, breathless. I look behind August to see his friend.

"Sorry to interrupt, kids," Colton says, not seeming sorry at all as he struts into the room—yes, struts.

When I go to slide off August's lap, he tightens his grip around my waist and I flinch. His eyes shift from the tray Colton places on the bedside table to me in a heartbeat.

"What was that?" August asks.

"Nothing," I tell him. "What's in the bowl?"

"I thought you might need a pick-me-up. I didn't know August was already giving you one." Colton winks. "Anyway, I made you tea. And by some miracle, this asshole actually had real food in his pantry for once so I made cereal salad." He smiles proudly at me.

Maybe I was too hasty in judging Colton. He seems like a totally different person when he's not trying to sleep with me.

"Cereal salad?" I peer over into the bowl. "Did

you mix Lucky Charms, Froot Loops, and Fruity Pebbles?"

"Yep, cereal salad," Colton confirms.

While I'm distracted by what looks like the best salad I've ever seen, August lifts the hem of my shirt, revealing my bare skin.

"Motherfucker," he curses as his fingers press along the bruised skin, his touch light as a feather. "I'm going to fucking kill him."

"I think you already did," I whisper.

"Why didn't you tell me you were hurt?" He stands, with me in his arms, and carries me into the bathroom.

"I'm fine. It's just a graze," I tell him.

"A graze you never should have fucking got. It's not fine, Hayley." August is mad. Although I don't think his anger is directed at me. No, it's at whomever's after him. "This is my fault."

"Someone trying to kill you? Probably your fault." I shrug. "Us being at the tree farm? That was my idea, my fault."

"Don't do that," August says, lifting my shirt again. I don't even think about what he's doing until the whole thing is over my head and tossed onto the floor.

"Do what?" I ask, suddenly self-conscious that

I'm sitting in front of him in just my shorts and a lacy bra. *Why didn't I wear a sports bra today?*

"Blame yourself." August moves to the cabinet and pulls out the first aid kit.

"Hayley, you're really missing out. This salad is delicious." Colton walks into the bathroom, bowl in hand.

"Get the fuck out. Now," August growls, standing in front of me to prevent his best friend from getting an eyeful, to go along with the mouthful of *my cereal* the bastard just downed.

"What'd I do?" Colton asks, unfazed by August's anger.

"She doesn't have a shirt on, idiot. Get out!" August yells.

"You're the one who took it off," Colton says before calling out to me, "Hayley, I'll be in the living room if you need anything."

I smile. "Is he always like that?"

"Unfortunately," August grunts. "This is going to sting. Sorry." He pours the antiseptic onto some gauze and then wipes over my wound.

I suck in a breath, because it does sting. "You know, it's just a graze. I'll be fine," I tell him.

August leans down and blows over the small

scratches, cooling the burn. Then he presses gentle kisses just over the bruise.

"Are you seriously trying to kiss it better?" I laugh.

"Yes." He peers up at me. "Is it working?"

I smile wider. Who would have thought that this big, bad monster would try to kiss me better?

"I'm not sure. I think you need to keep trying," I tell him.

August stands to his full height. His hands cup my face, tilting it upwards, and then he's kissing me. Not for show, not to fake it in front of cameras. No one is here to see and he's still kissing me.

Sure, when I kissed him on his bed, he returned it. But I thought maybe he was just being polite. There is nothing polite about the way he's kissing me now, though.

Chapter Eighteen

I'd hoped she'd come to me of her own free will. Although, when she kissed me on the bed, I thought it was just the fear, that she wanted something to anchor herself to. There's a possibility that that's still what this is. But she's kissing me, and I'm not going to stop it.

Fuck. I need to stop it. She needs to know what it means if we continue.

My hands travel down to her ass. Cupping each cheek, I pull her center hard against my cock. A small moan escapes her, and my fingers knead the flesh of her ass. With great remorse, I pull away from her mouth, but I don't let go of her. Instead, I keep her core pressed right up against my cock and slightly jut my hips forward.

"If we don't stop, I won't be able to," I tell her.

"What if I don't want you to?" Hayley asks, her voice breathless, husky. Her face flushed and her eyes glazed over with lust.

I tilt my head to the side, inspecting every inch of her. I need to be sure she wants this for the right reasons. "This isn't fake anymore, Hayley. I will keep you. This—us—if we keep going, you will be mine."

"Why would you even want that?" Her brows draw down in confusion. "August, you have a harem of women at your disposal. You really don't need to tell me sweet nothings. I'm okay if this is just... a holiday fling."

A holiday fling? Is she out of her pretty little fucking mind?

"You don't get it," I tell her.

"Don't get what?"

"You became mine the second I heard your voice on that phone. I've just been waiting for you to catch up with the program." I smirk at her, my fingers unbuttoning her shorts. "Now, I'm giving you the option here, babe. Do you need more time to catch up or are you ready to be mine?"

I lift her off the counter and drag her shorts and panties down to her ankles. Until I'm on my knees right in front of her, with her bare pussy on display.

Fuck. I need a taste. I know I said I was giving her a choice, but I didn't say I was going to make it easy for her. Spreading her thighs apart, I slide my tongue through her folds. Hayley falls backwards, leaning her elbows against the counter.

"I... oh god!" Her hands land on my head as I continue to explore her pussy.

"You what?" I ask, looking up at her. "What do you want, Hayley?"

"I want you to not stop. August, don't stop." She moans when my tongue circles around her hardened little bud.

"Tell me that you want to be mine, Hayley." Pushing two fingers into her opening, I curl the tips and rub against her inner wall.

"Yes. I want to be yours. Fuck!" Her body tightens as she comes around my fingers and mouth.

Then I stand and make quick work of freeing my cock. I drag her hips down until she's on the edge of the counter and step between her legs. Cupping her chin, I tilt her head up so that her eyes connect with mine. "Are you sure?"

"Are *you* sure? I'm a really bad girlfriend, August. I did warn you," she says.

"I've never been more sure of anything." Claiming her mouth with mine, I line up my cock with her entrance and slowly slide in. Stopping once I bottom out.

She's so fucking tight. I need to give her body time to adjust to the intrusion.

Hayley's legs wrap around my waist, her hands twist through my hair, and she pulls me closer to her. "Start moving, or I'm going to die," she whispers into my mouth.

With my hands firmly gripping her hips, I start pumping in and out of her. She feels so fucking good. So damn wet. I've never felt anything like this before. I look down to watch where our bodies connect and see why I've never felt anything like this. I didn't put on a fucking condom.

"Are you on birth control?" I glance back up at her face.

"Yes." Her answer both relieves me and pisses me off at the same time. She's on birth control because she's been sexually active. With other men.

Fucking hell, I shouldn't have asked.

I thrust faster. It doesn't matter who she was with before me. After today, I'm the only one she'll remember. I will fuck the others out of her head.

Hayley's body reacts to my increased pace, my harder thrusts. She likes being fucked hard. Bringing one of my hands up, I wrap it around her throat. My lips slam down onto hers, and I swallow the sounds of her moans. Her legs tighten around my waist, her ankles locked at my back.

Fuck me, I never want to stop.

Her pussy convulses, choking my cock as she comes again. Her nails dig into my scalp, and she screams into my mouth. Three more thrusts, and I'm following her over the edge, spilling myself inside her. Something I've never fucking done before.

Reaching behind me, I grab hold of her ankles and release the grip they have on me. I watch her pussy as I pull out, seeing myself spill from her. I scope my cum up from her thigh with a finger and push it back inside her.

"I've never done that before," I admit.

"What?" she asks.

"Come inside someone. It's fucking hot." I can't take my eyes off her. My fingers find the clasp of her bra and unclip it. I really should have done that earlier. I got so carried away.

"Shower?" Hayley says.

"Yes." I look at the time as I remove the watch from my wrist and curse under my breath. "Fuck."

"What's wrong?"

"I'm supposed to be at a fundraiser in two hours." I sigh.

"Okay, so shower and get dressed."

"I can't take you back out there, Hayley. I don't know what fucker is trying to get to me and I'm not going to risk you getting hurt again."

"That's why I'm here, to accompany you to these events, August. Let's just go. I'm sure it'll be fine. They're not going to try twice in the same day, are they?"

"They could. And that's not why you're here anymore. You're here because you're mine," I tell her.

Chapter Nineteen

Hayley

If I had known showers with August were so much fun, I would have jumped in a whole lot sooner. I don't think my body has ever been so thoroughly cleaned after being so thoroughly fucked. August left me alone to finish getting ready. This hair doesn't dry itself well. While I'm waiting for my curler to heat up, I send Jade a message. I need someone to talk some sense into me, because all my brain cells seem to go out the window as soon as I get in the same room as that man.

ME:

> What if the season of sin wasn't just for the season?

My phone rings almost immediately and I answer it on speaker. "Hey."

"You fucked him, didn't you? Of course you did. And now that you've had a taste, you want to keep the devil god," Jade grumbles into the phone.

"Actually, it's him," I tell her, as I start the process of curling the ends of my hair.

"What's him?" she asks.

"He wants to keep me." I sigh. I'm not sure if I should believe him. Why would he want to keep me? "He says it's not fake anymore, Jade, so what the hell am I doing?"

"Apparently a devil god." She laughs at her own joke.

"I'm serious! I'm in over my head here. You know what happens to me. I get attached and... that never ends well," I remind her.

"Okay, so it's not the German hottie Christmas fling we were planning. But tell me... was it good?"

"The best I've ever had," I whisper. Though I'm not sure why. No one is here. I'm sure August is busy out there with Colton, planning who knows what. "Oh god, I'm screwed, Jade."

"It would seem that way." Once again, she laughs at her lame joke. "Okay, it's not that bad. Let's think about this rationally. You're there because the ass backed you into a corner and didn't really give you much of a choice. He is the one saying he wants to keep you. That's not you, babe. And it's August Wade. Seriously, Hayley, even if he did break up with you, it's not like you would really be able to do anything. Because again, it's August Wade. If the guy didn't want someone getting close to him, they wouldn't be able to," she explains.

I would love to believe her, but I can't. He was just shot at today, and the other night, he was stabbed. People do get close, too close. And now all I'm thinking about is how I can keep him away from everyone else.

Shit, I really am spiraling. This is why I told him I wasn't a good girlfriend. I obsess. And that obsession turns into a light stalking here and there. I've had boyfriends I didn't even like that much and I still obsessed over them.

It's a trait I'm not proud of, and one I've avoided for a while by not dating at all. But now, it's happening again. I'm drowning in everything that is August.

"I don't know, Jade." I shake my head and try to steady my breathing. "You have to promise me something..."

"Depends on what it is..." she replies.

"If it happens, if I spiral too far, make sure you admit me again," I tell her.

She had to take me to the hospital for a psych evaluation when it got really bad. I was admitted for two weeks before the doctors released me, after deciding I wasn't a threat to myself or anyone else.

"Babes, you are fine. You're not spiraling. You're just in your post-orgasmic glow," she tells me.

"How's Riley?" I ask, quickly changing the subject.

"He's a pain in my ass, but he's been on his best behavior," she says. "So, how big we talking? Six? Seven?"

"I'm not telling you how big my boyfriend's cock is, Jade." I laugh, and then I see a pair of dark eyes staring right back at me through the mirror. "Ah, Jade, I gotta go. Talk later. I promise."

"*I promise,* she says," Jade huffs before adding, "Don't overthink it and have fun."

I cut the call and turn towards August.

"You look fucking breathtaking," he says, walking into the bathroom to stand behind me. I'm wearing a long black dress with a slit that runs up the left leg. The top is a halter neck and sits high. But the back, well, it doesn't exist.

"Thanks. I'm almost done," I tell him, curling the last of my hair.

"Take your time. I do have to apologize now, though," he says, his hands landing on my hips.

"For what?"

"Colton. He's coming to the fundraiser with us. Whatever he says, ignore him."

"I think I might like him. He's not that bad," I admit.

"Don't like him too much. I don't want to kill my only friend," August says.

"Okay." I smile.

I feel like I should just rip the Band-Aid off and tell him. He's bound to find out. Maybe if I do it now, it won't be so bad. He'll stop whatever this is and send me home. But then he could follow through on taking Riley's fingers, and I can't let that happen.

"What's wrong?" August asks me.

Pulling the hair curler out of the socket, I turn around. "I need to tell you something. You should know..." I start, my hands shaking. I've never admitted my problem to anyone other than Jade. I even managed to fool the doctors at the hospital into thinking I was just a scorned woman. I wasn't. I wasn't even heartbroken. I was just... obsessed.

"If you're about to tell me you have a boyfriend, or that you're married, *you should know* I will erase that problem. Permanently," August tells me.

Does he mean...? Surely he wouldn't kill someone just to make me single? I mean, I am single but...

I shake my head. "No, that's not it. I'm not seeing anyone."

"Hayley, next time you say that... next time someone asks you if you have a boyfriend, your answer should be: *Yes, and his name is August Wade.*" He smirks at me. "What is it, then?"

Chapter Twenty

Hayley walks past me into the bedroom. She's pacing up and down. Nervous. I wait. I don't reach out and take hold of her like I want to. I have no idea what kind of bomb she's about to drop on me. In my experience, when people are this nervous to tell you something, it's not good. So I lean against the wall, my hands in my pockets and my ankles crossed, and I wait.

"I told you I wasn't a good girlfriend. I wasn't joking, August. I'm really not a good girlfriend," she says.

"What makes you think that?" I ask her.

"I don't think it. I know it. I... I get attached really quick." She looks at me, waiting for a reaction. When she doesn't get one, she continues. "I become obsessed, August, like unhealthily obsessed with someone. I don't know where my limits are. I can't stop myself."

I smirk. She thinks her level of obsession is bad? She hasn't seen mine. "You're worried you're going to obsess over me, babe?"

"It's not funny, August," she says.

"I'm not laughing."

"I will become super clingy. I'm going to want to know where you are, all the time. I'm going to start calling and messaging—*a lot*—whenever you're not with me. Ever since my parents died, I've been like this. I can't let go."

"Okay." I shrug. I don't see what the problem is. "Hayley, you have a right to know where your boyfriend is."

"This is why I'm single. Because I've scared away every guy I've ever tried to date. I've done things I'm not very proud of," she whispers.

"Like?"

"Like once, I broke into an ex-boyfriend's house after he dumped me and slept in his closet because I needed to know when he came home. I needed to know he was there," she says. "I didn't even particularly like the guy, but I had this insane need to know where he was."

"Are you still fixated on these other guys, Hayley?" I ask her. Obsessing over me? No problem. But obsessing over someone else? Yeah, that's not gonna fly.

She shakes her head. "I've been single for two years, because it's easier to not get attached." She sighs. "But now, with you, it's starting again, August." Her words are meant to sound like a warning.

"Wait here." I walk into my closet and pull two air tags from my luggage. "Pass me your phone."

I hold out a hand. After installing the tracking program, I turn the air tag on and tuck it into my wallet.

"I will carry this on me at all times. You won't ever have to worry or stress about where I am, because you can log into here and see for yourself," I tell her. "I don't have anything to hide, Hayley. I don't care how much you call or message me. I don't care if you follow me around 24/7. In fact, I'd probably love that." I grin before passing her the second tag. "This one is for you. I want you to keep this on you, so I know where you are too."

Hayley pulls off her little silver necklace, threads the air tag on it, and clips it back in place before tucking the chain into her dress. "You're not worried?" she asks me.

"No. I'm not worried," I say. "If it ever feels like it's too much to handle, I want you to tell me. We can talk about it." I wrap my arms around her and pull her against my chest.

"You're supposed to be scary, a devil. A monster," she mumbles.

"To everyone else, I am." I laugh.

"Don't worry, I told Jade to admit me to the hospital again if I get too cray-cray."

"What do you mean again?" I ask. "And like fuck am I letting anyone shove you into a fucking hospital. There's nothing wrong with you, Hayley."

"I... I think we should just take it one day at a time," she says. "And we really should go to this thing of yours."

"Let's go. You got everything you need?"

"Mhmm." She nods her head.

"Holy shitballs, Hayles, babe, you look smokin." Colton's mouth drops open when we walk out into the foyer, where he's waiting for us.

"Colton," I growl.

"Sorry, boss, but she does." He shrugs.

"Thanks, Colton. You don't scrub up too bad yourself," Hayley tells him. "You do need a haircut, though. I could do it. Well, not now, but if you stop by the salon tomorrow or something."

"You're not touching his hair," I grunt.

"I can show you my portfolio. You do know I have my own salon?" She looks up at me.

"I know, but I'm not letting him get that close to you," I clarify. "You can cut mine no problem."

Hayley combs her fingers through the front of my hair. "Okay, but I like yours the way it is."

"You two are sickeningly sweet. I think I just got a cavity." Colton presses the button to call the elevator.

"That would be from the bowl full of sugar you ate," I tell him.

"Cereal is good for you," Hayley counters.

"That shit is not cereal, babe. It's sugar," I remind her.

"It says cereal on the box. So..." she *reminds me*.

"That's why you got normal food all of a sudden. We're keeping her," Colton says, pointing at Hayley.

I pull her tighter to my side. "I'm keeping her. You're keeping your eyes and hands off her."

"I did see her first. Wait... do you have a sister?" Colton turns to Hayley.

"No, but if I did, I would not let her near you." She laughs.

"Ouch, I'm a catch." Colton steps into the elevator.

"Have you ever let anyone *catch* you longer than a night?" Hayley quirks an eyebrow at him.

My friend's face scrunches up like he tasted something bad. "Why on earth would I do that?"

"Because you want a girlfriend?" she asks him.

"I don't want a girlfriend," Colton says. "I'm happy with my variety meal."

Hayley rolls her eyes before looking to me. "What is this fundraiser for?"

"To raise funds for the Davis Troubled Youth Foundation. They help young kids who find them-selves on the wrong side of the tracks," I tell her.

Hayley tilts her head to the side. "*You* are on the wrong side of the tracks, August. And I have no doubt Thing Two is right there with you." She gestures a thumb towards Colton.

I laugh. "We came up from the bottom, babe. Some of those kids have it worse than either of us ever did. But this is more about being seen and seeing the people I need to see than the charity itself."

"Okay. It's a good cause. It's just kind of ironic," she says.

Chapter Twenty-One

Hayley

"Do not open the door. You wait for me to tell you it's okay to get out," August says in a nonnegotiable tone. Honestly, if we hadn't just been ambushed earlier today, I would think he's overreacting.

I nod my head and wait. Anxiety creeps up as I stare out the window at August. He's the one they're after. He shouldn't be getting out first. My heart hammers against my chest. When I go to open the door, August steps in front of it. He then turns and opens it all the way and holds a hand towards me.

"Okay, we're going to be in and out, make our appearance, talk to who I need to talk to and then we're leaving," he says.

"Okay." I look down and flatten a palm over my dress.

"You look stunning," August tells me.

I don't feel it. I feel like a fraud. This is not my scene.

The moment we step into the ballroom and I spot all the beautiful, well made-up women, my nerves increase tenfold. My hand tightens around August's arm when a busty brunette approaches him. August looks across to me and presses his lips to the side of my head before greeting her. That tiny bit of reassurance, how did he know I needed that? Such a small gesture, but I can't wipe the smile off my face.

"I'm going to get drinks. Hayles, wanna come?" Colton asks me.

I shake my head. Is he insane? He wants me to

walk away and leave August alone with this woman? I can't do that. What if...

Shit, it's happening.

"Actually, I will come with you." I nod.

As I say this, August's hand tightens on my hip and his head snaps to the side. "You'll go where with Colton?" he asks me.

"To the bar. I'll get you a drink." Reaching up, I press my lips against his. I don't want to leave his side, but I have to. I need to not become that girl again. The girl who can't handle being away from her boyfriend.

"I'll take you there," August says.

"No, stay, finish your conversation. I'll be right back." I step out of his grasp.

Colton and Andre flank my sides as we approach the bar. I can't help but look back over my shoulder every few seconds to see if August is still where I left him. Every time I look back, he's looking right at me. Watching me.

"He's not going anywhere," Colton says.

"I know." I don't, but I want to believe it.

"So, Hayley, what are your intentions with my boy?" Colton asks, leaning one arm on the bar so he can get a better look at me.

"My intentions?" I repeat, my eyes continuing to flick back and forth.

"Yeah, I've never seen him so twisted up over a woman. This is the real deal for him, so if it's not that for you, then you should get out now. Actually, I think it's already too late. There is no getting out. You'll just have to find a way to fall in love with him." Colton shrugs.

"He is not in love with me." I laugh. That would be crazy.

"Isn't he?" Colton raises a single eyebrow and turns his gaze back to August. My gaze is already there.

"I mean, he can't be. He doesn't even know me," I say.

"I don't think love has anything to do with that. It's deeper, like a soul thing or something." Colton shrugs again before calling the barman over to place our order.

Is he right? Can you be in love with someone after just a few days with them?

"I think my intentions are to keep him." My eyes remain locked on August. He smiles back at me.

"You should probably know the guy can read lips." Colton laughs.

"I don't care. I don't have any secrets." I take the

offered glass of champagne from Colton, turning my glare his way. "Who is trying to kill him?"

"We don't know," Colton tells me. "Yet. We'll find them, though. We always do."

"So, this is a regular occurrence?" I ask.

"Not regular, but when you're at the top of the food chain, bottom feeders like to come out every now and then to try to make the climb."

"You really do need a haircut," I tell him. Changing the subject as I start to make my way back towards August, because it's been long enough. I walked away, and I didn't panic. Sure, I could see him the entire time, but I'm still counting it as a win.

When I reach August, he's quick to wrap an arm around my waist and pull me up against his side. "I don't like when you walk away from me," he whispers into my ear, and I shiver.

"I didn't walk away. I went to get a drink," I reply, sipping at the sweet champagne.

"Same thing," he grunts. "I like it better when you're within touching distance."

I want to tell him that he really shouldn't say things like that to me, because I will take it to mean more than it does. I will literally always be within touching distance, and that's not healthy for either of us.

My clutch starts vibrating, so I pull it out, frowning when I see the name of the local police station on my screen. Dread fills me. Last time the cops called me, it was to tell me that my parents were dead.

Oh my god, Riley!

"Shit," I curse under my breath.

"What's wrong?" August takes my phone, the one still ringing. He looks at the screen and answers it. "August Wade," he snaps into the receiver.

I don't hear what the other person says. All I can think about is my little brother. Where is he? Last time I tracked his location, which was only thirty minutes ago, he was at Jade's...

"This is her boyfriend. Whatever you need to tell her, you can tell me," August says.

I look up at him, my heart hammering against my chest. Everything blurs.

"We need to go." August pockets my phone a few seconds later.

"What happened?" I close my eyes.

Please don't be dead. Please don't be dead. I can't lose my only living relative.

"Riley was arrested. We need to go bail him out." August takes my hand. "Colton, I need you to stay, do the rounds."

"Sure thing, boss." Colton nods. "Don't worry, Hayles. August is a pro at bailing people out. He's done it for me more times than I can remember."

"He's been arrested. He's not dead." I look up at August, needing to hear it again.

His face softens. "He's just been arrested, Hayley. He's fine."

Chapter Twenty-Two

Since I can't kill him, because I don't think Hayley would be okay with that, I'm going to scare some fucking common sense into this kid. The look of sheer horror on Hayley's face when she received a call from the police department...

Fuck me, I do not want to see that look on her ever again. Her hand is gripped in mine tight. She's worried about her brother.

"He's okay, you know," I tell her.

"What if I had gone to Europe? I wouldn't be able to even get back here to help him. What was I thinking? I could have been in a completely different country. What if something did happen and I wasn't here? I should never have booked that trip. If I didn't, he never would have gone to your club. I never would have left him alone."

"We wouldn't have met," I remind her.

"There will come a day where you will wish for that too," she whispers.

"Doubtful." I chuckle.

"August, I almost couldn't handle walking to the damn bar in that ballroom without you."

She looks horrified at what she's admitting to me. Me? I fucking love that she wants to be near me all the time.

"The whole time, I thought something horrible was going to happen and I wasn't going to be there to stop it," she says.

That's her issue. She's not obsessed. She's

fucking scared of being out of control. Like when her parents died. Hayley told me this little "quirk" of hers started after their accident.

"Hayley, you've had a traumatic day. Give yourself a break," I tell her.

I need a way to make her happy. What the fuck can I do? I pull out my phone and message Colton.

ME:

I need a tree in my living room by the time we get back there.

COLTON:

Any tree?

ME:

A fucking Christmas tree, moron.

COLTON:

Do I look like Father Christmas?

ME:

No, more like an elf. Just make it happen. It's for Hayley.

COLTON:

Fine, but you owe me.

"Don't say anything when we go in there. If anyone asks you a question, do not answer it," I instruct Hayley.

"Why?"

"Because we don't like cops, babe." I smile. "Just let me handle this for you."

She nods, but I can see that she's skeptical. "We don't even know what he's done, August."

"Whatever it is, it's not going to be that bad."

"How do you know?"

"Because I've met the kid and he doesn't have it in him." I laugh. "He was scared shitless sitting in my office."

"You told him you were going to cut off his fingers. I'd be scared shitless too." She scowls at me.

"I would never do that to you. I don't want you to ever fear me, Hayley."

"I'm not scared of you. I'm scared of myself *around you*," she says.

"Come on, let's go get your brother out so I can beat some fucking sense into him." I sigh.

"How about we get Riley out and there is no beating involved?"

"It's a figure of speech, babe. I'm not going to touch your brother. Like I said, I would never hurt you."

I keep Hayley's hand firmly gripped in mine as we walk into the station. I fucking detest these places. "You got my kid brother—Riley Bell," I tell the cop at the front desk. He's new. It's obvious.

"Your name?" *See? Anyone else would know who the fuck I am without having to ask.*

"August Wade."

"Colton get dragged in again?" The familiar voice of Detective Greg calls out to me.

I smile. Fucker's on my payroll. "Not this time. Riley Bell, where is he?"

"Lock up. He one of yours?" Greg says.

"My brother," I repeat, and the detective quirks a brow.

"Since when do you have a brother?"

I don't answer. "Where is he?"

"I'll get him. Wait here." Greg looks from me to Hayley, who hasn't said a word.

A few minutes later, Riley is being escorted out from behind the locked door by the detective. Hayley lets out a gasp at the sight of him. Her brother's lip is split and his cheek is swollen and bruised.

"What the fuck happened to him?" I turn my anger on Greg.

"Got brought in for fighting. Charges have been dropped," Greg explains.

"Let's go." I don't wait for Riley to say anything. I turn and start tugging Hayley behind me, stopping when she lets go of my hand. I pivot and see her hug her brother.

"What happened?" she asks him.

"Hayley, not here," I tell her.

She glares at me and then looks back at Riley.

"It's okay. Let's go," Riley says.

It's not until we're in the car that I finally address the kid. "Who and why were you fighting?"

"My father's dead. I'm not looking for a new one," he grumbles.

"Good thing I'm not looking to fucking be one. Who did that to your face?" I ask again.

"Seriously, Hayley. This is happening?" Riley points to me and then to his sister. "I thought it was fake."

"It was," Hayley says. "Riley, what happened? Why were you fighting?"

"It doesn't matter," he groans.

"Riley, why?" Hayley's tone shifts from concern to authority. Her face telling him not to fuck with her.

"It was that fucking asshole, Shawn. He saw *you two*..." Riley gestures between me and his sister. "...making out on TikTok and said something about you. So I hit him. It's not a big deal."

"What'd he say?" I chime in. "About your sister?"

"He said if my sister was such a thirsty whore, he'd give her something to drink," Riley barks out.

My head snaps in his direction. "What the fuck? Where does this asshole live?"

"Don't answer that, Riley," Hayley interjects. "They're just words. You don't need to use violence to defend me against words."

"Yes, he does," I argue, and Riley smirks.

"No, he doesn't," Hayley scolds.

"Fine, he doesn't. But I will."

"No, you won't. Words don't matter. He's just a punk kid, August."

"I don't care if he's the fucking king of England. No one is going to talk shit about you," I growl.

"Andre, can you take us to Jade's? Riley is going back there," Hayley calls out to the front seat.

Andre looks to me, and I nod.

Chapter Twenty-Three

Hayley

After dropping Riley off at Jade's and giving him strict instructions not to leave, August told Andre to take us back to the penthouse.

"Why are you nervous?" August asks, pulling my

fingers away from my mouth. It's a bad habit. His hand clasps around mine and then he rests are joined palms on his thigh.

"I'm not," I lie.

August squints at me. "You know, I've never once lied to you, Hayley. I would appreciate it if you gave me the same courtesy."

Well, shit, now I feel even worse.

"I don't want to be a bother."

"Hayley?" August looks at me. Waiting.

"My salon isn't far from here. I was thinking I should stop in. I mean, I could stop in and check on things," I tell him.

"Andre, make a detour to Hayley's salon," August says before turning his attention back to me. "Why would you think that's a bother?"

"Because I've already taken too much of your time tonight. With Riley and everything." I mean, he was supposed to stay at that fundraiser. "You wanted me with you so you could attend these events and focus on business."

"That wasn't why I wanted you." August smirks. "It was just part of why."

When Andre pulls up to my salon without me having to give him the address, I raise a brow at August.

"I find out everything I need to know about someone," August says, answering my unspoken question before he gets out of the car.

Once he's satisfied that it's safe, he steps aside and holds out a hand to me. Then he guides me to the front door. I punch in the code and walk in, flicking on the lights.

"How would you feel about moving your salon closer to home?" August asks, following me inside.

I laugh. "Sure, because I can afford to lease a space anywhere near your apartment. Besides, this is close to *my* home."

He gives me a look I can't decipher but he doesn't say anything. Instead, he walks over and sits in the chair by the basin, and suddenly I have the urge to wash his hair.

I swipe up two towels and step up to his side. "Take off your jacket."

"Miss Bell, this your way of seducing me, because I gotta say... it's working." August winks at me as he shrugs out of his jacket. He then removes his tie and undoes the first few buttons of his shirt.

I tuck a towel into the back of his collar and around his shoulders, and push him backwards. "I want to wash your hair."

"Is it dirty?" he asks.

"No, I just like touching it." I smile and walk around to turn on the water. I wait for it to warm up before holding the nozzle over the top of his head. "Do you think Andre will mind having to wait?"

"Andre will do whatever he's told to do. It's his job," August says.

I squirt some shampoo onto my hands and start rubbing them all over his head, massaging his entire scalp.

August moans. "Fuck me, this is how you wash hair?"

"Mhmm." I focus on all the parts of his scalp that I know feel really good, turning the water back on before I wash the shampoo out, and then I repeat the process with a conditioner.

"Hayley?"

"Yeah?"

"How do you feel about quitting work altogether?" August asks.

"Why would I do that?" I laugh at him.

"Because I'm not sure if I can handle knowing you make other people feel this good all day." He groans as I dig deeper. I move my hands down over his shoulders, leaning over as my fingers move under his shirt.

"I don't wash anyone else's hair this good," I say, trailing kisses along his neck.

"Fuck me," August moans, grabbing hold of my hands. He somehow manages to pick me up and sits me on top of him. The split in my dress allows me to place my legs on each side of his. "Keep going."

My hands move back up to his hair, massaging the conditioner into his scalp. He really does have great hair. It's thick. Dark. And when it's wet, curls hang down over his forehead.

"I love your hair."

"I love your legs." August's hands travel up my thighs, and he pushes the fabric of my dress up over my hips.

His fingers then trail along my core. A bolt of pleasure runs through me.

"Don't stop," he says. "I want to fuck you, just like this." Shifting slightly, August undoes his pants and frees his cock.

Holy shit, this is happening. Never in my wildest fantasies could I have cooked up this situation.

I start rinsing the soap from his hair, and August pushes my panties to the side. His fingers explore my pussy before he slides two inside me. I'm already dripping wet for him.

"You want me to fuck you, Hayley? Right here?" he asks.

I nod my head. Because, well, I'm not an idiot and only an idiot would turn this man down.

August lines up his cock with my entrance, and then he pulls me onto his hips. His hands guide me up and down on his shaft.

"Oh god." I throw my head back, forgetting what I was doing. Water sprays all over both of us. "Shit." I reach forward to turn it off and then slam my lips onto his.

I start picking up the pace, fucking him, chasing the orgasm that's so close.

"Come for me," August growls against my mouth.

My entire body shudders, and August is right there with me, spilling his seed into me.

Chapter Twenty-Four

Throughout the entire ride back to my penthouse, I've been running over different scenarios on how to get Hayley to move her salon closer to me. That part of town isn't the best. I don't like the idea of her being there by herself. She was taking the week off, which means I at least have until after Christmas to come up with something.

When we walk into the penthouse, Hayley stops. Her jaw drops open and she gasps. "Holy shit!" she exclaims. Her hands shoot up to cover her mouth as her wide eyes turn to me. "What? How?"

I stare at the monstrosity that is taking up most of the floor space by the windows in the living room. The furniture has been moved aside to accommodate it. Fucking Colton... I asked him to get a tree, and the asshole had to go and get the biggest fucking one in the world.

"It's beautiful," Hayley says, walking up and tugging on one of the branches. "How did you do this?"

"I wanted to see you happy, so I called Colton and told him to make it happen."

"You did this for me?" she asks.

"Of course I did. Why wouldn't I?"

Hayley shrugs. "No one has ever done anything this nice for me. Well, no one other than Jade." She throws her arms around my neck. "Thank you. I love it."

"Good." I meld my lips with hers. The tree is

fucking huge. It's not something I would have picked, but if she loves it, it's not going anywhere.

"What're your plans for Christmas day?" Hayley asks.

"Unwrapping you and spending all day playing with my new favorite toy?" I quirk a brow at her.

"That sounds... fun. But since I'm in town, I was thinking I would go and see Jade and Riley."

"Invite them here for Christmas lunch," I tell her, because like fuck am I not having her here with me.

"Here?" Hayley glances around.

"Yeah, what's wrong with here?"

"What if we had lunch at my place?" she counters.

"What if this became your place?" What the fuck am I saying? Am I asking her to move in with me? I am, and I'm not taking it back.

"You... no." She shakes her head.

"What do you mean *no*?" No one says no to me. Ever. And why the fuck doesn't she want to live with me?

"You don't even know me that well yet, August. Also, I have responsibilities. They go by the name of Riley Bell. I can't just move in with you. What would I do with him? I won't leave my brother."

She's right. I wouldn't expect her to leave her brother.

"I realize you're a package deal, babe. Riley can have one of the spare bedrooms." Do I want to live with the kid? Fuck no, but I want *her* and if that means taking both of them, then that's what I'll do.

"You told me there weren't any spare rooms, August." Hayley looks around as if a guest room is just going to appear.

"I said there weren't any here *for you*, so there isn't. I want you in my bed. Our bed. Your brother's not invited into our bed, babe." I laugh. "Come on, let's go to sleep. We can discuss the details tomorrow. I'll arrange movers to get all your things packed up."

"I haven't said yes, August," Hayley tells me.

"You haven't said no either."

"Actually, that's exactly what I said," she huffs.

Bending at the waist, I pick her up and throw her over a shoulder. "We're going to sleep," I say, walking towards the bedroom.

Sitting across from Hayley at the dining table, watching her eat a bowl full of sugar, I can't help but smile. I could get used to this domesticated life. "What are your plans for today?" I ask her.

"I'm going to the salon. Need to get ready for the after-Christmas rush. And I need to pick up some gifts," she tells me.

"Didn't you take the week off from work?"

"Yes, but I was also supposed to be in Europe," she says.

"Want me to take you to Europe? I can have a jet ready in about five hours."

Her eyes widen and she smiles. "No, thank you. We just decorated this place, and I'm kind of excited to spend Christmas with Jade and Riley."

"Jade's baby daddy in the picture?" I've been meaning to ask that since I met the woman.

"No. Thank god." Hayley sighs. "He was a cheating son of a bitch."

"So she's doing it alone?"

"She's not alone. She has me," Hayley says. "I'm going to be the best damn aunt I can be."

"I have no doubt." I smile.

"What's on the agenda tonight?" Hayley asks me.

"You, me, and the bed." I laugh.

"No events?"

"Not tonight," I tell her.

"And what are *your* plans for today?"

"To find the fucker trying to kill me and make sure I kill him first." I shrug.

Hayley coughs. "Right, well, make sure you do."

"I'm going to be fine. I do have to go, though. Remember to call or message me as much as you like," I tell her. "Andre is downstairs ready to take you wherever you need to go."

"I don't need him to take me to my salon, August. It's a waste of his time."

"It's him or Colton," I say. "You choose."

"If I take Colton, I could at least give him that haircut he needs." She smiles at me.

"Nope, Andre it is." Leaning down, I kiss her forehead. "I'll see you later."

"Bye."

As I walk out the door, I think again about how domesticated this all is and how much I fucking like it.

Chapter Twenty-Five

I've been puttering around the salon for a few hours. I never really get the time to get in and give everything a really good once-over. I mean, the place is cleaned every day, but for the last few hours, I've reorganized all the cabinets. I've even managed to place an order for stock. It's been really productive.

The ringing of my phone blasts from my pocket. Plucking it out, I see Jade's name. "Hey, how's my niece doing?" I ask her.

"Well, I'm fine too, you know. I swear all I am to you these days is the vessel growing your niece." Jade laughs.

"Sorry. How's my niece's mama doing?"

"Good... Fat and hungry, always so damn hungry." She sighs, and I hear the crunching of what more than likely are chips. "What are you up to?"

"I'm at the salon. Just straightening some things up before next week. Oh, August said to invite you and Riley over for Christmas lunch, at his place," I tell her.

"Did he now? Why would he do that?"

"Because I told him I was going to your place. He wants us all at his," I explain. "Also, he asked me to move in with him, with Riley."

"And you said no, I hope."

"I did, but he doesn't really understand that word, Jade. He started talking about hiring movers and shit," I huff.

"Hayley, are you doing okay?" Jade asks.

"I actually am. I've been away from him all

morning, Jade. I've only checked his location four times," I admit, feeling good about this progression.

"And how are you checking his location?" she presses.

"He put an air tag in his wallet and the tracking app on my phone. Told me I can know where he is all the time because he doesn't have anything to hide from me." I've never been with someone as honest as August. It's refreshing and probably helping my anxiety and obsession levels a lot.

"So, he's just as nuts as you are, then? Good to know. Are you moving in with him?"

"I want to. But it's too soon. I know that."

"Fuck it, Hayles. If that's what you want, do it. But don't get rid of your house just yet," she tells me.

"I couldn't ever get rid of my house," I whisper. It belonged to my parents. Having it without any debt attached has been a godsend. We've never had to worry about having a roof over our heads.

"I gotta go pee. Again," Jade groans. "I'll call you back."

"Love you." As I pocket my phone, the bell on the door chimes. "I'll be out in a sec, Andre. I'm almost done!" I call out. I do feel sorry that he's had to wait outside the shop the entire time I've been in here.

When he doesn't respond, I stop what I'm doing and listen. The sound of heavy footsteps falling on my hardwood floors is all I hear. And those steps are getting closer to the back room.

"Andre?" I yell as I open the storeroom door. And right as I do, I'm shoved back by a man in a black ski mask. I go to scream but his hand comes up to cover my mouth.

"Shut the fuck up and listen, bitch, or I will cut your fucking throat," he hisses as he pushes me against the wall.

This is it. I'm going to die. My eyes widen and my entire body freezes. I know I should fight back, try to run out of this room, onto the street where there are people, but I can't move. Fear has me trapped.

"You're going to deliver a message to your boyfriend for me."

This is about August? Why?

"What do you want with him?" I manage to ask.

"He stole something. I want it back. Tell him he's got two days to give it back before I take everything he has, including his life."

The thought of this asshole killing August has me reacting. I shove against the guy's chest. "Fuck you, you won't touch him!" I scream.

"Fucking bitch." A hand connects with the side of my face.

I stumble backwards, hitting the shelves. That's when the guy lunges for me. The knife in his hand going into my stomach. I look down at my shaky, blood-covered hands before my masked attacker opens the door and runs out of the shop.

My knees collapse, and I fall to the floor. I reach into my pocket for my phone and hit Jade's number, close my eyes, and wait for her to answer.

Chapter Twenty-Six

I check the location of Hayley's air tag. She's still at her salon. She's not answering her phone and neither is Andre. Something isn't sitting well in my gut.

"I gotta go," I tell Colton.

"What's up?" he asks.

"Something's wrong. I can't get ahold of Andre or Hayley." I'm already walking out of the club and over to my car. We've spent all morning interrogating low-runners on the street, trying to get intel on who the fuck is targeting me. It took us going through twenty guys until we got one who would actually fucking talk.

Colton jumps in the passenger seat of my car. That's the thing about my best friend. As fucking annoying as he is, he is the first one there when shit goes down. Always having my back without me asking him to.

"I'm sure she's just busy doing whatever it is hairdressers do," he says.

"You ever get your hair done by a hairdresser?" I quirk a brow at him.

"I go to the same barber you do," Colton tells me.

"Hayley washed my hair last night. I'm never going to a barber again." I laugh.

"I'll have to book an appointment with her," Colton says.

"Over my dead body," I grunt. I know what he's doing. He's distracting me from the fact that I know something's wrong.

I don't know how many road rules I break to get

to Hayley's salon. The entire time, Colton tries to reach Andre without success.

As soon as we pull up out front, I spot Andre's car. He appears to be asleep.

"I'm going to fucking kill him..." I grumble under my breath as I jump out of the driver's seat. But when I get to the window, I see the blood splattered across the glass. Andre's head is slumped against the steering wheel. More blood is darkening his legs.

My head snaps up to the shop, and I run.

"No!" I yell, pushing through the door. "Hayley?" There's a dark red trail on the floor. I follow it to the back of the shop and shove the storage room open. "No, no, no!" My knees hit the ground as I fall next to Hayley's lifeless body. "Hayley, wake up, baby. Wake up." My fingers feel around her neck, and I thank God when they find a pulse.

"Fuck." Colton stands in the doorway. "I've called the ambulance. They're on the way," he says. He reaches above me, grabbing something off the shelf, and then lowers himself to the ground. "We need to stabilize this," he says, wrapping a towel around the knife handle.

His voice snaps me out of my fog. My first instinct is to yank it out. But we both been stabbed enough times to know better. Instead, I scoop Hayley into my arms, stand, and walk out into the main area of the salon.

"What the hell happened? Hayley?" Jade comes barreling through the door.

"Contain that," I tell Colton.

"*Contain that?* Fuck you! What the fuck did you do to her! I'm going to kill you myself, motherfucker." Jade lashes out at me, and Colton wraps his arms around her shoulders and pulls her away. "Get the fuck off me." Her head jolts backwards, connecting with his face.

"Fuck." He doesn't loosen his grip. "You need to stop before you hurt yourself. In case you forgot, you're a little bit pregnant," Colton tells her. "He didn't do this."

"I'm not pregnant, asshole. I just like to eat cake. Fuck you!" Jade attempts to throw her head back again, but Colton expects it this time and manages to dodge the blow.

And then the paramedics come rushing in with their gear.

"She has a knife wound to the abdomen," I say while carefully setting Hayley's body on the stretcher. My hand still holding the now-soaked towel around her wound. "You need to save her."

"Sir, you need to step aside. Let us do our job," one of them says.

"Her name is Hayley. Hayley Wade, my wife. I'm August Wade." I wait for recognition to sink in. She's not my wife, but if it will make these assholes care about actually saving her, I *don't care* about this lie. "If she loses her life, you'll lose yours," I tell them before stepping back.

"What the fuck!" Jade is still yelling.

One of the paramedics looks over at her. "Are you okay, ma'am?"

"My best friend has been stabbed. What do you think?" she hisses. Colton still has his arm wrapped around her. He's whispering something into her ear, the palm of his hand stretched out over her stomach, and then I watch her relax a little.

I follow the paramedics out to the ambulance and climb into the back. I'm not leaving Hayley.

"We'll be right behind you," Colton says, guiding Jade to the car.

I don't give a fuck if her friend hates me. Hayley is mine, and I'm not moving aside. I send up a prayer to anyone who could be listening, begging them to save her. I just found her, and I'm not losing her.

I am going to find the fucker who did this, and I'm going to fucking make them pay.

Hayley is rushed into an OR as soon as we make it to the hospital, and I'm left sitting in the fucking waiting room. Her blood all over me. This is my fault. Whatever happened to her is because of me. I'm aware of this, and yet I'm still not prepared to let her go.

"Who would do this?" Jade asks, her voice much quieter now. She sounds defeated.

I don't answer her. I don't think it would help her if I did.

Chapter Twenty-Seven

Hayley

eep, beep, beep.

What is that? My eyes blink open, only to shut tight again when I'm blinded. Trying to sit up, I squint against the light and then stop moving when a searing pain rips through my stomach.

"What?"

"Hayley, babes, it's okay. Don't move. I'm right here."

Jade's here. I sink back down into the bed.

"What happened?" I ask. And then I remember, and my eyes shoot open. "August. Where is he?" I look around the room. I'm in the hospital and he's not here.

"Hayley, calm down." Jade pushes on my shoulders when I try to sit up.

"August!" I yell as loud as I can. "I need to find him, Jade. I need to find him." I shake my head.

What if that guy's already gotten to him? I didn't warn him. I need to find him.

"He's coming back. He just stepped out. He'll be back," Jade tells me.

"Where's my phone?"

"I don't know." She shakes her head. Then she takes out her own phone, presses a button, and puts it to her ear. "She's awake and she's screaming for you, asshole," she says before passing the device over to me.

"August?" I ask.

"Babe, you're awake. I'm sorry I had to leave. I'm coming back. I'm on my way back," he says.

"You're okay?" I ask him.

"I'm okay. You're going to be okay."

"He... August he said... he wanted something from you," I attempt to explain.

"I know. He isn't a problem anymore, Hayley. No one is going to hurt you ever again. I promise," he says. "I'm almost back. Colton is there."

I look around the room. I don't see him, but then the door opens and the man in question struts inside. "Huh, you're awake. Thank fuck." Colton sighs.

"He's here," I say into the phone.

"Hayley, I... I'll see you real soon, okay?" August quickly cuts the call.

"He's okay." I rest my head against the pillow and pass the phone back to Jade.

"I changed my mind, Hayley. You shouldn't move in with him. You need to cut ties. Look where you are? It's been two fucking days and you were already attacked because of him."

"It's not his fault some psychotic asshole stabbed me," I grumble.

"Yes it is," she says.

"No, it's not," I growl before I shift my attention

to someone who doesn't hate August. "Colton, where did he go?"

"He had an errand to run, babe. He'll be back annoying the fuck out of both of us before you know it," he says. "You hungry? Want me to go find something?"

"I don't think you're going to find any cereal salad here." I smile at the memory.

"Pfft, I can find anything I want, anywhere I want, babe." He winks at me.

"Her name is Hayley, asshole. Use it." The growl from the doorway makes me smile wider.

"You're here," I state the obvious.

Ignoring everyone else, August walks over to me. He bends down and presses his lips to mine. "How are you feeling?"

"Better now that you're here," I tell him. Jade scoffs, and I look around August's large frame to glare at her. "Can you go get me a drink? Something besides water, please?"

"What do you need?" August stands, ready to go and fetch me whatever I want. I take hold of his hand to stop him.

"Jade will get it," I tell him, my eyes glued to my friend.

"Fine, but I might or might not spit in it," she

mutters, and I laugh.

"I'll come with you." Colton follows Jade out the door.

"Thank god she's pregnant." I laugh.

"Why?" August asks.

"Because I don't have to worry about Colton hitting on her," I tell him.

"You think her being pregnant would stop him? She's a female. I can guarantee he's already hit on her." August shakes his head, a smile spreading across his face. Then he lowers himself onto the edge of the bed, lifts my hand to his mouth, and gently peppers it with kisses. "I'm so sorry this happened."

"It's not your fault."

"It is," he says. "I never should have let you go out alone."

"I wasn't alone. Andre was there." I glance around the room, realizing I haven't seen him since the salon. "Where is he? Where's Andre?"

"He's... Want some water?" August stands and goes to the table where there is a jug and a glass.

"August? Where's Andre?" I repeat.

"I don't want to say, and I'm also not going to lie. So please don't ask." He doesn't look at me as he pours some water into the cup.

"Where is he?"

"He's gone, Hayley. We found him... It was too late to help him," August whispers.

Tears start running down my face. I only knew him for a few days. But August knew him, trusted him. "I'm so sorry."

"You didn't do this, so you don't have to be sorry," August says, coming back over to the bed.

"No, I'm sorry that you have to feel that pain. He was your friend."

"Nothing will ever compare to what I felt watching you bleed out on the ground. That... I've never been more scared in my life, Hayley."

"Can I go home?"

"Not until the doctor says you can."

"Can you lie with me, then?" I shuffle across the bed, and August climbs in next to me. "I'm scared to go to sleep."

"Why?"

"Because I don't know if you will be here when I wake up," I tell him.

"I'll be right here. I promise I'm not going anywhere." August kisses the top of my head, and I let my eyes close.

Chapter Twenty-Eight

TWO HOURS EARLIER

"**I** got him," Colton says, looking up from his phone.

We've been sitting in the hospital room, waiting for Hayley to wake up. The doctor said he was able to stabilize the bleeding, so there shouldn't be any long-term effects—thankfully, the knife missed anything vital.

"Where?" I'm already standing, ready to go.

"You stay here. I'll go get him," Colton says.

"No, he did this to my girlfriend. Not yours. You stay here. Call me the second she wakes up," I tell him. "Send me the details."

I walk out the door and force myself to keep going. I want to stay with her, but I need to find the fucking asshole who did this to her. I need to make sure he can never touch her again. And there's only one way for that to happen.

By the time I get to the car, I've got the details on my phone. I tap the address into the GPS. It's a twenty minute-drive.

Good, I can be there and back before Hayley wakes up. Hopefully.

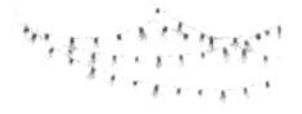

I pull up two houses down from the fucker who I've now learned is Joseph fucking Kenn. A guy Colton and I grew up with. What the fuck he thinks I stole from him, I have no idea. It doesn't matter, though. The minute he went after Hayley, he sealed his fate.

I open the glove compartment, take out the pistol I keep there, and check that it's loaded. Then I walk up to the door. I don't knock. Instead, I kick the fucker down and storm inside—gun raised.

"Drop it," I tell him when I turn and see Joseph reaching for his own weapon.

He looks at me and then at the gun. I quirk a brow. *Really, motherfucker? You think you're going to be faster than I am.*

"You went after the wrong fucking person," I grunt.

His hand is still hovering above the gun. "Fuck you, August. You took what's mine," he spits out.

"Yeah? And what's that, exactly?"

"You stole my life. You're living my life. It was

supposed to be me. It was my idea. The drugs, the club. You stole my fucking life, asshole," he says.

"You're a fucking moron. You want my kingdom?" I swing my free arm out to the side. "Take it."

The second his hand reaches for the gun, I shift my aim and pull the trigger. A bullet goes right through his wrist, and he screams.

"Did she scream? When you stabbed her, did she fucking scream out in pain?" I ask, taking a step closer to him.

"Fucking bitch was only worried about you," he hisses out. "She didn't care what I did to her."

My hand moves, the barrel of the gun now aimed at his head. "See you in hell, motherfucker." I pull the trigger, three times, because I want to make sure this asshole is really fucking dead before walking out as quickly as I'd entered.

I look up and down the street. I don't even care if anyone sees me. No one is going to say shit. Not in this neighborhood.

I'm about five minutes away from the hospital when my phone rings.

"She's awake and she's screaming for you, asshole," Jade's voice spits out through the phone, and then I hear her. *Hayley*.

I slam my foot down on the pedal. I need to get back to the hospital now. I didn't want her to wake up without me being right there.

Chapter Twenty-Nine

Hayley

It's Christmas morning. I was able to go home last night. Both Jade and Riley came with me to August's penthouse. I guess it's *our* penthouse?

He is insistent on calling it *our home*. It took

some convincing to get Jade to agree to come. In the end, I told her that he made me happier than I've ever been. And she caved. She's still not August's number-one fan, but that's okay, because that spots already taken by me. And Jade? She's always going to be my best friend.

"Morning." August walks into the bedroom holding a mug.

"Is that coffee?" I ask.

"It is."

"Oh, thank god! I think I love you." I take the cup from his hand, and August's body freezes.

"*You think?* I know I love you, Hayley Bell." He sits next to me on the bed. My heart hammers in my chest.

"You shouldn't tell me that, August," I warn him.

"Why not?"

"Because what if hearing it makes me... I don't know... too clingy?" I ask him.

I'm so stressed about reverting to my old stalk-erish behaviors. August, however, seems to welcome my level of crazy.

"Cling away. I don't care." He leans down and kisses me briefly. "Merry Christmas," he says, handing me a small box.

"Um?" I don't know what to say. My hands shake

as I open the box. Somewhat relieved and slightly disappointed when it's not a ring inside. "A key?" I have no idea what it's for.

"It's symbolic. You have the key to my heart. The key to our home. The key to our future," he explains.

That is way better than a ring.

I smile up at him. "Thank you so much. I love it."

August eyes me for a moment. "You thought it was going to be a ring."

I start to shake my head, but his whole *no lying* policy stops me. "It's a small box, and when a man hands a woman a small box, she always thinks it's a ring, August."

"What would you have said? Out of curiosity? If it were a ring?" he asks me.

"I don't know. I would probably tell you that it's too soon, and you would tell me it's not soon enough or some crap like that, and then you'd tell me you've already picked a date." I laugh, because that seems like something this man would actually do.

"Good to know your answer would be a yes." He smirks. "You ready to face the heathens out there?"

"Our friends are not heathens." I laugh again.

"Yours, maybe. Colton most certainly is," August says with all seriousness.

When we walk out—very slowly with August

supporting most of my weight—Colton is the first one I see. "Breakfast. Merry Christmas." He hands me a bowl filled to the top with milk and cereal.

"Thank you," I reply as August helps me onto one of the sofas. I lean over and whisper into his ear. "I love you too. I forgot to say it back. But I don't think. *I know.*"

He takes hold of my face and his lips slam onto mine. His tongue pushes into my mouth, and I get lost in him.

"Gross. That's my sister." Riley's voice breaks through my August fog, and I pull away.

"Merry Christmas, Rye." I'm about to stand when he holds up a hand to stop me.

"Don't get up." He bends over and hugs me. "Merry Christmas, sis. You feeling okay?"

"I'm good," I tell him.

Ever since he found out I was stabbed, he's hardly left my side. I know it scared him and reminded him of when our parents died. We are all we have. Well, I guess now we have August too.

"Okay, present time!" I squeal.

This is my favorite part of Christmas. Giving. I look across to Jade, who is curled up on the other sofa rubbing her protruding stomach. She smiles back at me, and I just know everything is going to be okay.

August takes hold of my hand.

"Colton, you can play Santa. Pass out those gifts," I tell him.

"This body is far too toned to be Santa," Colton grumbles.

"I don't know... Hot Santas are *in* at the moment." Jade laughs.

"Ew. Don't," I warn her, knowing that she won't. At least, I don't think she would...

I can't wipe the smile off my face as I look around at everyone gathered in this room. This isn't the European Christmas of my dreams. It's better than that. It's more... It's family.

What's next in the KylieVerse?
Dead Or Alive - Emmanuel And Evie's Book, a standalone dark cartel romance.

Dead or Alive

Emmanuel

Love is a weakness.
You either kill it, or it will kill you.
I've been in love once, I killed it.

I've managed to avoid the weakness my entire life.
And then I saw her. The very thing I killed.
Not dead, and very much alive right in front me.
When she tries to flee from my grasps, I hold tighter,
Because dead or alive, Evie is mine.

Evie

I've spent my life being put on display.
Beautiful, a word I've heard a million times.
Do I believe it? No.
I might be shiny and pretty on the outside, but the
inside...
It's a dark, scarred and bruised place.
When I wake up to a cartel boss looming over me,
dark eyes, a jaw clenched tight,
My first instinct is to reach out and comfort him.
That's where I realise my mistake.
But it's the one word he utters, that has my skin
crawling. "Who?"
He knows...He can see the ugly.

About the Author

About Kylie Kent

Kylie made the leap from kindergarten teacher to romance author, living out her dream to deliver sexy, always and forever romances. She loves a happily ever after story with tons of built-in steam.

She currently resides in Sydney, Australia and when she is not dreaming up the latest romance, she can be found spending time with her three children and her husband of twenty years, her very own real life instant-love.

Kylie loves to hear from her readers; you can reach her at: author.kylie.kent@gmail.com

Let's stay in touch, come and hang out in my readers group on Facebook, and follow me on instagram.